"So this is it," Luc whispered.

"We're married," Kelly whispered back.

"You may kiss the bride," the officiant said.

Luc did so, intending it to be light and easy, but somehow he couldn't quite pull away from her. He was aware of everything about her: the sweetness of her scent, the warmth of her skin, the feel of her mouth against his.

When he finally broke the kiss, he felt thoroughly flustered. And she looked as if she felt exactly the same way.

Dear Reader,

When a prince wants to be a heart surgeon rather than a king, and a cardiologist wants everyone to stop matchmaking, the solution to both their problems is a marriage of convenience.

But love has a way of turning up when you're not looking for it. And when Luc and Kelly try to make everyone believe they're having a whirlwind relationship when they're really just good friends, they find that life might just have a surprise in store for them…

I hope you enjoy Luc and Kelly's story. They had a surprise in store for me, too, because they decided to elope to New York. But I had a lot of fun researching it…

With love,

Kate Hardy

HEART SURGEON, PRINCE...HUSBAND!

KATE HARDY

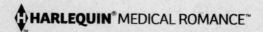

Recycling programs
for this product may
not exist in your area.

ISBN-13: 978-1-335-64139-7

Heart Surgeon, Prince…Husband!

First North American Publication 2019

Copyright © 2019 by Pamela Brooks

Printed in U.S.A.

To Sheila Crighton, a wonderful friend,
with love and thanks for the lightbulb.

CHAPTER ONE

'LUCIANO BIANCHI, the new heart surgeon, is starting today,' Sanjay, the head of the cardiac unit, told Kelly. 'Can I ask you to look after him for me this morning—take him round the department, show him where the canteen is and introduce him to everyone? I'd do it myself, but I've got meetings with suits.' He rolled his eyes. 'All day.'

'Oh, the joy of budgets,' Kelly said, sympathising with her boss. 'Of course I'll show him around.'

'Wonderful. Thank you.' Sanjay patted her arm.

Rumours had already flown around the hospital. Luciano Bianchi wasn't just a cardiothoracic surgeon; he was a *prince*. His father was the King of Bordimiglia, a small Mediterranean country on the border between Italy and France. Apparently he'd trained in London and worked for some years at the Royal

Hampstead Free Hospital; now one of the surgeons here was retiring, Luc was moving to Muswell Hill Memorial Hospital.

Everyone had looked him up on the Internet, of course; it was hard to reconcile the idea of an upper-class playboy who didn't take life too seriously with a man who'd spent years training to be a heart surgeon. So who was Luciano Bianchi—and would he be part of the team or would he be a royal pain in the backside?

From the photographs, he was definitely nice-looking enough to make all the women in the department sigh and speculate why he hadn't been snapped up years ago. Tall, with dark hair and dark eyes, Luciano looked more like a model for a high-end fragrance ad than a surgeon. But he didn't seem to date that much—or, at least, there weren't loads of paparazzi pictures of him with a princess or the daughter of some wealthy industrialist on his arm, on their way to some high society party or movie premiere. It looked as if he put his job before his position in society, which boded well for life at the hospital.

Kelly wasn't one for gossip, but one rumour that had caught her attention involved his work. He was allegedly going to set up a trial for a new surgical procedure to help patients suffering from hypertrophic cardio-myopathy—a condition where the muscular wall of the heart thickened and made the heart stiff, making it harder to pump blood around the body.

It was too late for a trial to help Simon; but it wasn't too late to help his younger brother Jake or Jake's daughter Summer.

Kelly would never forgive herself for the fact that she hadn't picked up on her late husband's heart condition. How could a trained cardiologist have missed something that massive? Since then, she knew she'd become a workaholic—but she was determined that nobody's symptoms would go unrecognised on her watch. She didn't want other families to have to go through what her family had been through. And getting Jake and Summer onto the trial might help to blunt the edges of her guilt. If she explained the situation to Luciano Bianchi, then maybe she could persuade him to at least consider Jake and Summer as candidates for his trial.

She kept an eye on the reception area from the office where she was catching up with paperwork, and twenty minutes later Luciano Bianchi walked through the doors. She pushed her chair back and went out into the reception area to greet him. 'Mr Bianchi?'

He turned to look at her. 'Yes.'

Oh, help. Maybe she should have called him 'Your Highness'. But he was here in his capacity as a surgeon, not as a prince, so she'd used the convention that surgeons were called 'Mr' rather than 'Dr'. She summoned up her best smile. 'I'm Kelly Phillips, one of the cardiologists,' she introduced herself. 'Sanjay is stuck in meetings all day, so he's given me a reprieve from paperwork to show you round and introduce you to everyone. And, if you don't have any other plans, to take you to the canteen for lunch.'

Luc was used to people judging him first as a prince and secondly as a doctor, but maybe at last his reputation at work was starting to take precedence, because Kelly Phillips was definitely treating him as a surgeon and a colleague. He really liked the fact that she'd called him 'Mr Bianchi' rather than 'Prince Luciano'. And, OK, there was an unobtrusive bodyguard with him, because of who he was, but his security detail was discreet. Luc didn't want to be treated any differently from the other staff on the team. He was here to save lives, just like they were. A doctor first and a prince second: and he thought he could serve his country far better with his medical skills than by doing the job he'd been born to do but his older sister would do so much better.

'Thank you. That would be good,' he said, holding out his hand to shake hers. 'Nice to meet you, Kelly. I'm Luc.'

'Nice to meet you, too, Luc. Welcome to the department.'

She shook his hand, and it felt as if he'd been galvanised. He really hadn't expected to react so strongly to her, with his skin actually tingling at the contact with hers.

Then he shook himself.

Even if she wasn't already involved with someone, Luc had no intention of letting his relationship with Kelly Phillips become anything other than professional. Until the situation with his father was resolved, it wouldn't be fair to start dating anyone. He'd already learned the hard way that women who dated the prince didn't want to date the doctor, and vice versa. The two sides of his life sat uneasily together, and all his relationships seemed to fall through the fault line.

'Thanks for the warm welcome,' he said.

'It's a Muswell Hill Memorial Hospital tradition. First stop, staff kitchen,' she said. 'Though I'm afraid it's instant coffee and a kettle, here, rather than a posh coffee machine.'

Uh-oh. It sounded as if she was starting to

see the prince rather than the surgeon. 'Which makes it much easier to add cold water so you can drink the lot down in one,' he said with a smile. 'Between the operating theatre, seeing my patients and drowning in paperwork, I'll take my caffeine any way I can get it. Instant's fine.'

She looked relieved at the reminder that he was just like any other doctor. 'And there's a treat shelf. Patients and their families are always bringing in biscuits or cake for us.'

'And then they wince and apologise for buying something so unhealthy, given that half of our patients have been given dietary advice to cut back on sugar and fat?' Luc asked with a smile.

'I suppose it's like taking a big tin of chocolates to a gym at Christmas,' she said with a grin. 'Though we're just as grateful for the goodies as the personal trainers are.'

Because sometimes, after a rough shift, when you'd tried everything and it still wasn't enough to save your patient, cake and a team hug were the only things that could help stop you falling into a black hole. However much professional detachment you had, losing a patient was always grim. 'Yes,' he said softly.

'I assume you've already been given your

computer login?' she asked. 'If not, I'll ask Mandy to chase it up for you. She's officially Sanjay's secretary, but she keeps an eye out for the rest of us. She knows everyone and everything, so she's the fount of all knowledge, and we keep her in flowers because she keeps us all sane.'

'I'll remember that,' he said. 'Yes, thanks, I've got my login, my staff ID and my lanyard.'

'Pick up your locker key from Mandy, and you're good to go.' She smiled at him again. And he was going to have to ignore the way his pulse rate kicked up a notch when she smiled.

The more he heard, the more he liked the sound of his new department. And all his new colleagues turned out to be as warm and friendly as Kelly, instantly accepting him as one of them rather than being slightly suspicious of Prince Luciano's motives For working in a hospital rather than a palace.

'I think we're both due in clinic now,' Kelly said when she'd finished introducing him to everyone, 'but I'll meet you back here in Reception at one for lunch. Patients permitting.'

'Of course,' he said. 'Thank you for showing me round.'

* * *

That handshake had thrown her.

Ever since Simon's death, Kelly had kept all her relationships strictly platonic, and she hadn't so much as looked at another man; she barely joined in with conversations in the staff kitchen about the latest gorgeous movie star. It was partly because she wasn't ready to move on; and partly because the whole idea of starting over again with someone, falling deeply in love with them and then risking losing them, was too much for her.

The sensible side of her knew that what had happened with Simon was rare—a life-threatening genetic condition that usually showed symptoms, but in his case it hadn't. The chances of dating another man with hypertrophic cardiomyopathy were small; the chances of dating another man with HCM who had absolutely no symptoms of chest pain, light-headedness or breathlessness were even smaller. So minuscule as to be absolutely unlikely.

But.

She could still remember the numbness and shock she'd felt when she'd taken that phone call, two years before. The way her life had imploded, as if in slow motion; she could see it happening but could do nothing to stop it.

The sheer disbelief that her husband—the man who cycled to work every day, did a five-kilometre run every Sunday morning and loved playing ball with their nephews in the park—had collapsed and just died. They hadn't even had the chance to say goodbye; and it was her big regret that they'd waited to start trying for a family. Simon was a brilliant uncle and he would've been a great dad. He'd just never had the chance.

For the last six months, Kelly had been fending off well-intentioned matchmaking by her family and friends, urging her to go out on a date and have fun, because Simon wouldn't have wanted her to be on her own for the rest of her life; he would have wanted her to be loved. She knew that; just as, if she'd been the one to die, she would have wanted Simon to find someone to share his life with and love him as much as she had.

But she just wasn't ready to move on. She couldn't forgive herself for not picking up on his HCM. She was a cardiologist; she'd treated quite a few people with Simon's condition and she knew all the symptoms. There must have been something she'd missed. Something she should have spotted. She'd let the love of her life down in the worst possible way. And she wasn't going to let any of her patients down.

She blew out a breath. And it was ridiculous to let Luciano Bianchi throw her. Absolutely nothing could happen between them. OK, so he seemed to be dedicated to his career; but even though he didn't have the lifestyle of a ruler-to-be, that was exactly what he was. The heir to the kingdom of Bordimiglia. No way would he be allowed to get involved with anyone who didn't have a single drop of blue blood in her veins. He'd end up marrying a princess for dynastic reasons. His relationship with her was strictly business. And that little throb of awareness when his skin had touched hers—well, she was just going to ignore it.

She managed to focus on her patients for that morning's clinic; and Luc's clinic clearly ran on time as he was waiting for her in the reception area at one o'clock.

'Hi. How was your first morning?' she asked brightly.

'Fine, thanks. We have a good team,' he said with a smile.

A smile that shouldn't have made her feel as if her heart had just done a backflip. She pulled herself back under control. Just.

'How was your morning?' he asked.

'Good, thanks,' she said. 'It was mainly follow-up appointments today, and it's always lovely to see your patients gaining in confidence, once they've had time to come to terms with their diagnosis and started to make the lifestyle changes that will help them.'

'I know what you mean.' He smiled. 'We held a yearly party for the heart transplant and bypass patients at the Royal Hampstead Free. It was great to see them all dancing and making the most of the time they didn't think they would get with their families.'

'That's such a nice idea,' she said. 'Maybe Sanjay will let us set up something like that here.' She walked with him to the canteen. 'It's your first day, so this is my shout—and don't argue, because it's a departmental tradition.'

'As long as I get to take the next new recruit under my wing and pay that forward,' he said.

'Deal.' She grinned. 'I think you're going to fit right into the team, Luc.'

He nodded, looking hopeful.

'The food is all pretty good here, and the coffee is decent,' she added.

They'd just sat down to eat their sandwiches when Kelly's phone pinged to signal an incoming text.

'Sorry to be rude,' she said, 'but do you mind if I check my messages? It's probably my sister Susie—she's due her twenty-week antenatal scan today.'

'And you should have been meeting her for lunch instead of babysitting me?' Luc asked.

She smiled. 'No, she's being seen in a different hospital. Even if we'd arranged to meet halfway, I would only have had time to say hello and give her a hug before I had to rush back here for clinic.'

'Then go ahead and read your message,' he said. 'You're not being rude. If it was one of my sisters in that situation, I'd want to know how the scan went, too.'

'It's probably just a round robin telling everyone it's fine, or she would have phoned instead of messaging me,' Kelly said. But she checked her phone anyway, then grinned. 'Yup. All's well, and she and Nick decided not to find out whether it's a boy or girl.'

'Is it her first baby?'

'Her third—she already has twin boys.'

'Twins run in your family, then?' he asked.

She shook her head. 'On Nick's side—her husband. Oscar and Jacob have just turned five, and I think she's hoping for a girl this time so she gets to do ballet as well as football. Do you mind if I just send her a quick reply?'

'Of course not.'

She tapped in Great news, love you. X—and

then her phone pinged to signal another message from Susie. Kelly didn't bother reading beyond the first line because she knew exactly what her sister had in mind.

'Answer that as well, if you need to,' he said.

'It can wait.' Kelly grimaced. 'I love my sister dearly, but I swear since she's been pregnant...'

'Older sister bossing you about?' he guessed.

'Trying to.' She sighed. 'Actually, you might as well hear it from me, than from someone else in the department who means well. My husband died two years ago, at the age of thirty. He was cycling to work when he had a cardiac arrest. The paramedics couldn't save him, and the coroner's report said he had HCM. It was a complete shock because he'd had no symptoms whatsoever.'

'But, as a cardiologist, you think you must've missed something?' Luc guessed.

Kelly swallowed hard. 'I've been over and over it in my head, trying to see what I missed, and he really *didn't* have any symptoms. His dad died young from a heart attack, but his dad had a high-stress job, plus he smoked and drank too much; everyone assumed his heart attack was because of all that and they didn't bother doing a post-mortem. I guess because of what happened to his dad, Simon was more aware of heart health than the average person, even before he met me. He didn't smoke, he drank in moderation, he ate sensibly, he cycled to work and exercised regularly. He did everything right.'

Yet still he'd died. And how she missed him. Why, why, why hadn't she joined the dots together and made him go for that all-important check-up that would've spotted his unusual heart rhythm? Why hadn't she made the connection about his father? Why hadn't she thought there might be more to his father's heart attack than his lifestyle?

'My sister, my mum and my friends have all decided that I've been on my own for long enough and they're forever trying to fix me up with a suitable potential partner,' she continued. 'That's why Susie's asking me to go over to dinner tonight. She says it's so she can show me the scan pictures, but I know she'll also have invited someone that she thinks is perfect for me.'

'And you're not ready?'

'I'm not ready,' she confirmed. 'I know they all mean well, but it drives me crazy and I can't seem to get them to back off. I loved Simon and I know he wouldn't have wanted me to be alone, but...' She sighed. 'Sorry. I didn't mean to dump all that on you. What I was really going to ask was if the rumours are true about you running a trial for HCM patients, and if so whether you were looking for people to join the trial?'

'Because you have a patient who might be suitable?'

She wrinkled her nose. 'Not my patient, but I do know two people. Simon's younger brother Jake, and his daughter Summer—she's four. After Simon's PM, I nagged Jake to get tested just in case there was a faulty gene involved, and unfortunately I was right. Which also makes me think they inherited the condition from their dad—except obviously there aren't any medical records to back that up.'

'And Summer has inherited the gene too?' Luc guessed.

'Yes. With a family history that spans at least two generations—and I'm pretty sure if you went back there would be more—they'll be good candidates. And you'll get a spread of age and gender.'

Even though Kelly was clearly devastated by her husband's loss, she was still thinking about his family and trying to help them, putting their needs before her own, Luc thought. He could certainly talk to their current medical practitioner and see if they would be suitable candidates for his trial.

But something else Kelly had said struck a chord with him. Maybe, just maybe, they could help each other out. He'd had a crazy scheme percolating in the back of his head for a while now, but he hadn't found the right person to help him. Maybe Kelly was the one; she was in a similar kind of position, so she might just understand his problem.

He was normally a good judge of character and he liked what he'd seen of Kelly Phillips so far; her colleagues had spoken highly of her, too. So maybe it was time to take a risk—after he'd had the chance to check out her background and got to know her a little more, because he wasn't reckless or stupid enough to ask her right at this very second. 'If you can ask their family doctor to contact me, we'll go through all the prelims and see if they fit the criteria,' he said.

'Thank you. I really appreciate that,' she said.

'It's not a promise that it will definitely happen, but it's a promise that I'll do my best to help,' he said.

'That's fair.' She smiled at him. 'So did you train at the Royal Hampstead Free?'

'Yes, and I loved working with the team

there. But then this opportunity came up, so I applied for the role,' he said. 'How about you?'

'I trained here,' she said, 'and cardiology was my favourite rotation. I love the area, too, so I stayed. What made you become a cardiac surgeon?' she asked, sounding curious. Then she grimaced. 'Sorry. Ignore me; that was a bit rude and pushy. You really don't have to answer.'

'It goes with the territory. Given who my family is, most people expect me to be part of the family business rather than being a medic.' He shrugged. 'That's what probably would have happened—but my best friend, Giacomo, died when we were fifteen.' He winced slightly as he looked at her.

'From a heart condition?' she guessed.

He nodded. 'I'm sorry if this opens any scars, but yes—the same one as your husband.'

'HCM.' Three little letters that had blown her world apart.

'It wasn't genetic, in Giacomo's case. His family doctor thought the chest pains were just teenage anxiety because Giacomo was worrying about his exams.'

She blinked. 'Chest pains in a teenager and the doctor didn't send him for tests?'

'No. Knowing what I do now, I wish he had.

His condition would've shown up on the ECG, and then medication or an ICD might've saved him. But hindsight is a wonderful thing.' He shrugged. 'Giacomo was playing football at school with me at lunchtime when he collapsed and died. The teachers tried to give him CPR but they couldn't get his heart started again.'

She reached across the table and squeezed his hand for a moment, conveying her sympathy. 'I'm sorry. That must've been hard for you.'

'It was. He was the brother I never had.' And it had shocked him profoundly to come face to face with his own mortality at the age of fifteen. Giacomo had been the first person he'd ever known to die, and the fact it had happened in front of him had affected him deeply. Not wanting to feel that way again, he'd put up a slight emotional wall between himself and everyone he loved. 'I'm reasonably close to both my sisters,' he added, 'but we don't talk in quite the same way, with Eleonora being two years older than I am and Giulia being five years younger.'

'So you wanted to save other families going through what your best friend's family went through?'

Just what he suspected she was trying to do,

too. He nodded. 'Becoming a doctor pretty much helped me to come to terms with losing him. And I like my job—bringing people back from the brink and giving them a second chance to make the most of life.'

'Me, too,' she said.

When they'd finished lunch, they headed back to the cardiac ward together.

'Thank you for lunch,' Luc said.

'Pleasure. I might see you later today—if not, see you tomorrow and have a good afternoon,' Kelly said.

'You, too,' he replied with a smile.

And how bad was it that he was really looking forward to seeing her?

CHAPTER TWO

ON TUESDAY MORNING, Kelly was due in to the cath lab. Her first patient, Peter Jefferson, looked incredibly nervous, and his knuckles were white where he was gripping his wife's hand.

She introduced herself to them both. 'Come and sit down. I promise this looks much scarier than it is. I'm going to check your pulse and your blood pressure, Mr Jefferson, and then I'll put a little plastic tube called a cannula into your arm. Then all you have to do is lie on the couch for me, hold your breath and keep still for a few seconds, and the scanner will take 3D pictures of your heart so I can take a look at what's going on. Then we can talk about it and decide the best way to treat you to stop the chest pain. Is that OK?'

He nodded.

'I'm going to inject some special dye into your veins to help the scanner take the pictures. It'll make you feel a bit warm and you might notice a funny taste in your mouth, but that's completely normal and it'll only last for about thirty seconds,' she reassured him.

'And it's not going to hurt?' He was still gripping his wife's hand.

'It's not going to hurt,' she said. 'If you're worried about how you're feeling at any stage, just tell me. I might need to give you some medicine called a beta-blocker to slow your heart down very slightly, or some GTN spray under your tongue to make the arteries in your heart get a little bit wider—that will help me get better pictures of your heart. But it won't hurt,' she promised.

'It's just the chest pain has been so bad lately,' Mrs Jefferson said, 'and the medicine our family doctor gave him doesn't help.'

Angina that couldn't be helped by medication often meant that the arteries were seriously narrowed, and the treatment for that could mean anything from a simple stent through to bypass surgery under general anaesthetic. Hopefully a stent would be enough, but she wasn't going to worry him until she could review the scan pictures.

She gave them both a reassuring smile. 'Once we've gone through the tests, I should have a better idea how to help you. Can I just check that you've stayed off coffee, tea, fizzy drinks and chocolate yesterday and today, Mr Jefferson?'

He nodded.

'And he's been eating better lately and stopped smoking,' Mrs Jefferson added.

'Two of the best things you can do,' Kelly said. 'OK, Mr Jefferson. When you're ready, I'll check your blood pressure.'

As she'd expected, the first reading was really high; a lot of patients were so nervous about the tests that it sent their blood pressure sky-high. By the third reading, he was beginning to relax and Kelly was a little happier with the numbers.

Once she'd put the cannula in, she asked Mr Jefferson to lie on the scanner couch with his arms above his head. 'I'm going to put some wires on your chest now,' she explained, 'so I can monitor your heart rate during the scan, but again it's not going to hurt.'

But she really wasn't happy with what the scan showed her. His right coronary artery was severely narrowed, as were the two on the left. An angioplasty with a stent wasn't going to be enough to make any difference.

'I'm sure your family doctor has already explained why you're getting chest pain, Mr

Jefferson, but I'd like to go through it with you again. Basically your heart pumps blood round your body, but sometimes deposits of fat and cholesterol—what you might hear called plaques—stick to the wall of your arteries and make them narrower. It's kind of like when you see the inside of a kettle in a hard water area and the pipes are furred up, except in this case the furred-up bits are inside the pipes rather than outside. This means not enough oxygen-rich blood gets through to your heart, and that's why it hurts.'

'But you can make my arteries wide again?' he asked.

'I was hoping I could do an angioplasty and put a stent in—that's basically a wire mesh that I can put inside your arteries to keep them open,' Kelly said. 'But in your case there's a lot of narrowing in three of your arteries, and I think your best option is surgery. I need to talk to one of my colleagues—the cardiothoracic surgeon—very quickly, so if you'll excuse me I'll be about five minutes. If you'd like to nip out to the waiting area to get a cup of water while I'm gone, please feel free.'

To Kelly's relief, Luc was in his office, dealing with paperwork.

'Can I have a quick word about one of my patients?' she asked.

'Sure.'

She drew up Peter Jefferson's scan results on the computer. 'My patient has angina, and the meds his family doctor prescribed aren't helping. I hoped that I might be able to do an angioplasty, but I'm really not happy with the scan results. I think he needs a CABG.'

'I agree. That narrowing is severe. I'd recommend a triple bypass,' Luc said as he reviewed the screen. 'Is he still with you?'

'Yes. He's in the cath lab with his wife. He knows I'm having a quick word with you.'

'Let me check my schedule.' He flicked into the diary system. 'Operating days for me are Wednesday and Friday.' He blinked. 'I've got a cancellation tomorrow, by the looks of it, so we can grab that slot now before someone else does. Do you want me to come and have a word?'

'Meeting you is going to reassure him more than anything I can say to him,' Kelly admitted. 'Would you mind?'

'No problem.' He smiled at her.

And her heart *would* have to feel as if it had done an anatomically impossible backflip because of that smile.

Kelly had got herself completely back under control by the time they went into the cath lab.

'Mr and Mrs Jefferson, this is Luciano Bianchi, one of our surgeons,' she said. 'We've had a quick discussion, and we both feel that the best way forward is surgery—a coronary artery bypass graft.'

'It means I'll take another blood vessel from your leg and attach it to your coronary artery on either side of the bit where it's blocked—that's the graft—so the blood supply is diverted down the grafted vessel.' Luc drew a swift diagram.

'I guess it's a bit like roadworks, when you get diverted down a slightly different road round the bit that's blocked. Your blood will flow through properly to your heart again and you won't get any pain,' Kelly said.

'Exactly,' Luc said with a smile.

'But what about the bit in his leg? Doesn't he need that vein?' Mrs Jefferson asked, clearly looking worried.

'It's one of the extra veins we all have close to the surface of the skin,' Luc said. 'The ones that return the blood back to the heart are deep inside your leg. The rest of the veins in your leg will manage perfectly well if I borrow a little bit for a graft, Mr Jefferson. I'll stitch it up and you'll have a little scar, but it's nothing to be worried about.'

'Heart surgery. Does that mean you have to cut through my chest?' Mr Jefferson asked.

'In your case, yes—unfortunately I can't do keyhole surgery for you because you need three grafts,' Luc said. 'It means you'll have a scar down your chest, but that'll fade with time. And once I'm happy with the grafts, I can re-join your breastbone with stainless steel wires and stitch up the opening.' He smiled. 'And I happen to have a slot free tomorrow morning, so I can fit you in then.'

'Tomorrow?' Mr Jefferson looked utterly shocked.

'Tomorrow,' Luc confirmed. 'Which gives you less time to worry about the operation.'

'Surgery.' Mr Jefferson blew out a breath. 'I wasn't expecting that.'

'I've done quite a few bypasses in my time,' Luc reassured him. 'You won't feel a thing, because you'll be under a general anaesthetic.'

'Isn't that the operation where you'll stop his heart beating?' Mrs Jefferson asked. 'I read up about that on the Internet.'

'It's one way of doing a bypass operation, using a heart-lung machine to breathe and pump the blood round your body for you, but actually I prefer to do my surgery off-pump—

where the heart's still beating while I operate,' Luc said.

Kelly hadn't expected that, and it intrigued her.

Mr Jefferson's eyes widened. 'But isn't that dangerous?'

'It's quicker, so you'll be under anaesthetic for less time, there's less chance of you bleeding during surgery, and you're also less likely to develop complications after the operation,' Luc said. 'So in my view it reduces the risks.'

'And after the surgery you'll be with us in the ward,' Kelly said. 'You'll be in Intensive Care at first, where we'll keep an eye on you to make sure everything's working as it should be. You'll still be asleep for the first couple of hours, but then we'll wake you up and your family will be able to see you.'

'You'll be well enough to get out of bed and sit in a chair, the next day,' Luc said. 'A couple of days later you'll be back on your feet, and a couple of days after that you'll be ready to tackle stairs again.'

'A whole week in hospital.' Mr Jefferson looked as if he couldn't take it in. 'My doctor said I'd be in here for half an hour, maybe a bit longer if you had to do a procedure like a stent. He didn't say I'd have to stay in for a week.'

'But if you need the operation, love,' Mrs Jefferson said, 'then you'll have to stay in.'

'I'm afraid you do need the operation, Mr Jefferson,' Luc said gently. 'Right now I know it feels very scary and a bit daunting. But it's the best way of preventing you having a heart attack.'

'But our daughter's having a baby next month,' Mr Jefferson said.

'Which is another reason to have the operation now. You'll be able to cuddle the baby without worrying that you'll start getting chest pains,' Kelly said. 'By the time the baby's crawling, you'll have made a full recovery and can really enjoy being a grandad.'

'And you won't be left to deal with everything on your own afterwards,' Luc added. 'Heart surgery is a big operation, and we'll help you recover on the ward.'

'You'll come back to us a few weeks after the operation to start a rehabilitation programme,' Kelly said, 'and that will help you get completely back on your feet. There are support groups, too, so we can put you in touch with other people who've already been through the same thing—they'll understand how you're feeling and can help you.'

'And it's really bad enough that I should

have the operation tomorrow?' Mr Jefferson asked.

'Your arteries are severely narrowed,' Luc said. 'Right now that's causing the pains in your chest, and the medication isn't enough to stop the pain. But on top of that there's a risk that one of the plaques will split and cause a blood clot that will completely block the blood supply to your heart and give you a heart attack. That could do a lot of damage to your heart muscle.'

'And kill him?' Mrs Jefferson asked.

'We always try our best to save our patients but, yes, I have to tell you that's a possibility,' Luc said. 'I know it's a lot to take in, but we'd really like to keep you in overnight here and do the bypass tomorrow, Mr Jefferson.'

'So will the operation cure him completely?' Mrs Jefferson asked.

'It will stop the pain and lower the risk of having a heart attack,' Luc said.

'But because you have coronary heart disease you'll still need to look after your heart,' Kelly added. 'Your family doctor's probably already told you what you need to do. Stopping smoking and eating better are brilliant, so definitely keep that up, and maybe add in a bit more gentle exercise.'

Mr Jefferson still looked terrified. 'I hate

needles. I can't even make myself give blood, even though I know I ought to. Coming here today for this was bad enough.'

Kelly held his hand. 'I know it's scary now, but in the long run you'll feel so much better. And your wife and daughter won't have to worry about you as much as they do now. Luc's really good at what he does, and so is the rest of our team. It's natural to feel worried, and you'll probably feel a bit wobbly at times after the operation—that's absolutely normal. But the operation is really going to help you. You're going to feel a lot better, and you're not going to worry that your chest pain or breathlessness is going to stop you playing with your grandchildren.'

'Are there risks?' Mrs Jefferson asked.

Luc and Kelly exchanged a glance.

'There are risks with all anaesthetic and surgical cases,' Luc said. 'But they're small, and we're experienced enough to know what to look out for and how to fix things. I know it all sounds really daunting, but there's a greater risk if we don't do the surgery.'

Mr Jefferson swallowed hard. 'All right. I'll do it.'

'Good man.' Luc rested his hand briefly on the older man's shoulder. 'We'll get you settled in to the ward, and I'll be doing rounds later if you have any questions. Dr Phillips will also be on hand if you need anything.'

'Or talk to any of the nurses,' Kelly added. 'That goes for both of you.'

'Thank you,' Mrs Jefferson said.

Once Mr Jefferson was settled on the ward and had been put on a nitrate drip, Kelly went back to the cath lab. The rest of her clinic was more straightforward, to her relief, and she managed to catch up with Luc afterwards.

'Thank you for talking to Mr Jefferson with me.' She'd liked Luc's warm, easy manner and the way he'd described things without being dramatic and terrifying their patient even more. He'd acknowledged Mr Jefferson's fears and reassured him.

'No problem,' he said.

'You actually do the surgery off-pump?'

He nodded. 'I'm assuming that's unusual for here, then?'

'Yes, it is. I haven't actually seen off-pump surgery done before.' And it was the first time in a long time that Kelly had been interested in seeing something different—that her old passion for her job had resurfaced instead of being buried by the fear that she might have missed something and let a patient down, the way she'd let Simon down.

'If you can spare the time, you're welcome to scrub in and observe as much of the operation as you like,' he offered.

'I'd love to. I won't be able to stay for the whole thing, but maybe I could come before or after my clinic tomorrow, if that's OK?'

'Whenever fits your schedule best,' he said.

'Thanks. I'm definitely taking you up on that.'

'Actually, you can spread the word that I'm always happy to have observers,' Luc said. 'The actual operation is only a part of caring for our patient. I'm a great believer in all areas of the team knowing exactly what happens in the other parts of a care plan, and the more we all understand what each other does, the more we can work together and help our patients.'

'That's very much Sanjay's approach as the head of the department,' Kelly said. 'Cross-fertilisation of ideas. And you're welcome in my cath lab any time, as are any of your students.'

'Thanks. I'll take you up on that.' He smiled. 'So is Mr Jefferson settled in?'

She nodded. 'His wife's just gone home to pick up his things. She had a bit of a chat with me beforehand. She's worrying about losing him.'

'Understandable, in the circumstances,' Luc

said. 'But that must've brought back some tough memories for you.'

She shrugged. 'If anything, what happened to Simon has probably helped me empathise a bit more with my patients and their partners.' There had to be *some* good coming out of such a senseless death.

'You're still brave,' Luc said, patting her shoulder.

Again, his touch made her feel all flustered. Which was crazy. She hardly knew him and this wasn't supposed to happen. 'You have to get on with things,' she said.

As if realising that she desperately wanted him to change the subject, Luc said, 'So Mr Jefferson's on his own and he's got time to worry, then. I'll go and sit with him for a bit. Catch you later.'

Surgeons had a reputation for arrogance, Kelly thought, the next morning, but Luc Bianchi definitely wasn't one of them. Yesterday he'd deliberately taken time to sit with a nervous patient and reassure him. Today, he was courteous to the rest of the team in the operating theatre, asking them to do things rather than barking instructions at them, and even checking that they were OK with his choice of music to work to; and he'd made it clear that he was happy to explain anything he was doing and why.

She was fascinated by the glimpses she had of the off-pump bypass surgery where just the small area he was working on was kept still and the rest of the heart was visibly pumping. As a student, she'd been fascinated by cutting-edge treatments. Since Simon's death, she'd focused on keeping things safe and steady. Work hadn't been a chore, exactly, but she'd become hyper-focused. She managed to be there for the end of the op too, when Luc was closing up; his movements were deft and very sure.

'Thanks for letting me sit in,' she said before he went to scrub out. 'Can I buy you lunch and ask you a ton of questions about the op?'

'I'd be delighted to have lunch with you and answer anything I can,' he said, 'but I'm paying. I might have to rush back here if the team beeps me too.'

In other words, if Peter Jefferson developed any complications before he came round in the intensive care unit. 'Of course,' she said. 'Thank you. I'll see you when you've scrubbed out.'

The more time Luc spent with Kelly Phillips, the more he liked her. The kind, calm way she treated her patients; her inquisitive mind; the way she treated all her colleagues with respect.

'Was that really the first OPCABG you've seen?' he asked when he'd scrubbed out and joined her.

'Your predecessor preferred working on pump,' she said. 'So, yes, it was my first off-pump bypass graft. And it was fascinating.'

'And you have questions?'

'Absolutely. Let's get lunch, and I'll pick your brain,' she said with a smile.

She asked a lot of questions. All bright, thoughtful questions. Luc answered to the best of his ability, and finally she nodded.

'Thank you. I understand a lot more, now. But the most important thing is that you've made a real difference to Peter Jefferson's life.'

'We're not quite out of the woods yet,' he said. 'But I hope so.'

Over the next couple of days, Peter Jefferson moved from the intensive care area to the ward. But, when Kelly came to see him on Friday morning during her ward round, he started crying. 'This is so pathetic. I can't understand why I feel like this. I was a finance director, used to making decisions and dealing with huge sums of money, and now I'm crying all over the place and it's just not me. And I can barely even get out of bed without help.' He looked despairing. 'Now I'm just a shuffling old man.'

She sat on the bed next to him and held his hand. 'You've been through major surgery, Mr Jefferson. Lots and lots of people feel like this afterwards. You'll have good days and you'll have wobbly days. But the rehab programme will really help you, because you'll meet other people who are going through it too or are a couple of weeks further down the line than you are, and that will help you realise that what's happening to you and how you're feeling is all perfectly normal. It's going to take time to get you back on your feet and doing the same things you did before you had surgery, but you *will* get there. Just be kind to yourself.'

Luc walked onto the ward at that moment. 'Good morning,' he said with a smile. 'I just popped in to say hello to you before I go into the operating theatre today.'

Mr Jefferson wiped his eyes. 'I'm sorry. I'm being so stupid.'

'You've had major surgery with a general anaesthetic. Of course you feel wobbly,' Luc said. 'Tell me, do you play chess?'

'I do.'

'Good. I'll get a board sorted out and I'm challenging you during my lunch break. I might be a bit late,' he said, 'depending on how the operation goes this morning, but I'll definitely be in to have a cup of tea and a chess match with you, OK?'

'But—you'll have been so busy this morning.'

'And a game of chess is the perfect way to relax,' Luc said. 'As long as you don't mind me eating a sandwich at the same time. I'm horrendously grumpy if I don't eat regularly.'

'Thank you, Dr Bianchi. That's—that's so kind of you.' Peter Jefferson wiped his eyes again.

'I'll see you soon,' Luc said, patting his hand.

'I need to see my next patient,' Kelly said, 'but I'll pop back later, too.' She walked out with Luc. 'That's really nice of you.'

'I just want my patients to be comfortable.' He shrugged. 'I don't suppose there's a chess board on the ward?'

'Probably not, but I might be able to borrow one from Paediatrics. I'll get that organised—and a sandwich for you. What would you like?'

'I eat anything, so the first thing you grab

off the shelf will be fine,' Luc said. 'Thanks, and I'll settle up with you later.' He paused. 'Are you at the team thing tonight?'

'The ten-pin bowling? No, I'm working. Are you?'

'Yes. I thought it'd be a good way to get to know the team.'

'It is.' She smiled. 'Have a good time.'

'Thank you.'

To her relief, he didn't push to see if she was going to any of the other team events. She liked her colleagues very much—but going out was a strain. Too many people trying to push her into being sociable when she was really much happier here at work, making a difference to her patients' lives.

Luc spent the morning in Theatre fixing an aortic aneurysm on an elderly woman, his lunchtime with Peter Jefferson, and his afternoon in Theatre sorting out a narrowed aortic valve in a teenage boy suffering from severe breathlessness.

By the time he got to the bowling alley, he was glad of the chance to let off steam. Though he learned from his colleagues that Kelly hardly ever joined team events nowadays. Because she was still mourning her husband? He needed to tread carefully.

He didn't see her again until Monday morning. 'How was your chess match?' Kelly asked.

'It was fine,' he said. 'I think Peter was glad of the company. He was beating himself up a bit because he was shuffling, and just taking those few little steps exhausted him.'

'Two days before that, he was in Theatre, having major surgery. He's doing brilliantly,' she said.

'That's what I told him. I said that my patients always worry that it'll take ages to get fully back on their feet, and at the same time they're terrified of overdoing things in case it makes them have a relapse. How he's feeling is how all my patients feel.'

'I'll make sure I reassure him about the rehab sessions,' Kelly said.

'I assume it's the same as we did at the Royal Hampstead Free—an exercise programme tailored to the patient and graded so they can see their progress?'

She nodded. 'Plus there will be plenty of professionals there, he'll have a monitor attached during the exercises so we can keep an eye on his heart rate, his blood pressure and his pulse. The team will help each patient progress at the right pace for them, and their safety is paramount.'

'Good,' he said. 'Did you see your sister's scan photo, by the way?'

'Yes.' She took a photograph from her wallet and handed it to him. 'They're going to call the baby Reuben if he's a boy, and Emma if she's a girl.'

'Lovely.' His fingers accidentally touched hers, and again he felt that inappropriate zing. To stop himself thinking about it, he asked, 'So were you right and Susie had someone lined up to partner you at dinner?'

'Yes, and he was very sweet and very charming. He understood when I explained that it wasn't him, I just don't want to date.' She grimaced. 'My best friend's doing exactly the same thing this weekend. She's arranged pizza and tickets to a stand-up comedy thing for a group of us, and I know I'm going to end up sitting next to the eligible single man in the group. I know they love me and they mean well, but...' She shook her head. 'Sometimes I'm so tempted to invent a fake boyfriend, just to get them to back off.'

A fake boyfriend?

That wasn't so very far from the marriage of convenience he had in mind.

'Maybe you should,' Luc said carefully.

She wrinkled her nose. 'Except then they'd insist on meeting him. And it's not really fair to ask someone to—well, be my fake boy-friend and lie to everyone for me.'

She could ask me, Luc thought—or maybe I can ask her. He wanted to get to know her a little better first, but he was beginning to think they really could help each other. 'If you explained the situation to someone suit-able, I'm sure he'd be happy to help you out.'

'Really?'

For a second, he thought she was going to ask him, and his heart actually skipped a beat.

But then she spread her hands. 'I might think about that a bit more. But thank you for the male insight.'

If he nudged her to think about it a bit more, then hopefully she'd be receptive when he finally asked her a similar question…

CHAPTER THREE

OVER THE NEXT couple of weeks, Luc found himself working with Kelly on their patients' care between the cath lab and the operating theatre, where she needed to do the investigations and liaise with him about potential surgery. The more he got to know her, the more he liked her. The way she put everyone at ease, the way she told terrible jokes, the way she made the day feel brighter just because she was in it.

In other circumstances, he would've been so tempted to ask her out on a date. But she'd told him she wasn't ready to move on after losing her husband, and he had a political tightrope to walk in Bordimiglia. So he'd enjoy her friendship and he'd just have to start mentally naming every blood vessel in the body, from the internal carotid artery down to the dorsal digital artery, to stop himself thinking of anything else.

But on Sunday afternoon his eldest sister called him.

'Is everything OK, Elle?' he asked. He and Eleonora usually managed to grab a few words during the week, but there was something slightly antsy about her tone.

'Ye—es.'

'But?'

'Babbo wants to start taking things easier. He told me yesterday that he's planning to step down at some point in the next year,' Eleonora said.

Meaning that King Umberto was expecting his wayward son to give up his job as a surgeon, come home and take his rightful place on the throne? So the clock he'd pretty much managed to ignore, thanks to its silence, had just started to tick. 'Is that Elle-speak for "come home right now"?' he asked wryly.

'No, I'm just putting you in the picture so you know what our father's thinking. He'll probably summon you home to talk about it at some time in the next month, though,' Eleonora warned.

Summon him home. Normal people of his age were happy to visit their parents; whereas Luc knew a visit home wouldn't be time to catch up with each other and enjoy each other's company. It would be another chance for his father to nag him about his future in the monarchy, and he'd end up having another argument with his father. He sighed. 'Elle, you and I both know you'd make a better ruler than I would. So does our father. And you're the oldest. It's ridiculous. This is the twenty-first century. It makes absolutely no sense that, even though I'm second-born, I should be the heir just because I have a Y chromosome.'

'It's how things are.'

He could hear the resignation in her voice. 'Well, things need to change. It's time our father modernised the monarchy.'

She sighed. 'I hate it when you fight.'

'Elle, I'm a cardiac surgeon. I've spent half my life either studying to become a doctor or practising medicine—and I'm good at what I do. I can make a real difference to my patients and their families, give people a second chance at life. That's such an amazing thing to be able to do. And I want to stay here for a couple more years, get experience in all the cutting-edge surgical developments. Then I can bring it home to Bordimiglia and set up a world-class cardiac centre.' And he'd name it after his best friend. So Giacomo would never be forgotten.

'Giacomo would be proud of you,' Eleonora said softly. 'His parents think you're wonderful.'

Whereas his own parents thought he was being stubborn and unreasonable. They'd given him the freedom to do what drove him, so far, but now it seemed the pressure was going to start in earnest: they'd want him to go back to being a prince instead of a surgeon. But that wasn't who he was. He could serve his country much better as a surgeon. Make a real difference to people's lives.

'I really hate all the fussiness of protocols and politics, Elle. If I become king, I'll make a dozen horrible gaffes in my first week, and we all know it. Whereas you're a born diplomat.' Though even Eleonora hadn't been able to talk their father into changing a certain tradition.

'Sometimes you have to pick your battles wisely. This isn't one we're going to win, Luc.'

Unless he did a little shaking up himself.

He'd talk to Kelly. Hopefully she'd agree with him that they could do each other a favour and his plan would work. 'Leave it with me,' he said.

'No fighting with Babbo,' Eleonora warned.

'I know. Mamma hates it when we fight, too, and so does Giu. And it's not that much

fun for me, either. I'm not arguing for the sake
of it. Don't worry, Elle.' He switched the conversation to how his niece and nephew were
doing, and his sister sounded a lot less strained
by the end of the call than she had at the beginning.

When he'd hung up, he went through the
dossier on Kelly that the palace PR team had
quietly compiled for him. There was nothing
the press could use to pillory her, so she'd be
protected. There might be a bit of press intrusion, to start with, but it would soon die
down because he knew that he was too quiet
and serious and frankly *boring* to make good
headlines.

He'd talk to her on Monday.

Luc spent Monday morning in clinic. His first
patient, Maia Isley, had Marfan Syndrome—
a genetic connective tissue disorder which
caused abnormal production of the protein
fibrillin, so parts of the body stretched more
than they should when placed under stress.
It was a condition which needed help from a
variety of specialists, as the patient could develop scoliosis, have loose and painful joints,
and suffer from eye problems. From a cardiac
point of view, Marfan Syndrome could also

cause problems with the aorta being enlarged, so patients needed regular check-ups and a yearly echocardiogram where the team could look at the structure of the heart and measure the size of the aorta.

Luc had already compared the new scan that Kelly had just performed to last year's, and he wasn't happy with the differences.

'How are you feeling, Mrs Isley?' he asked.

'Fine,' the young woman replied. 'But, from the look on your face, you're expecting me to feel worse than usual, right?'

Luc nodded. 'Obviously you've learned a lot about your condition, so you know there's a risk of your aorta—the biggest artery in your body, the one that starts at the top of the pumping chamber in your heart—getting wider, and that can make blood leak back into your heart so your heartbeat starts pounding and you get breathless.'

Maia shrugged. 'My heartbeat feels like it normally does.'

'And also there's a risk of the aorta tearing.'

'If it tears, I die, right?' Maia asked.

'There's a high chance, yes. Your aorta's grown wider since last year. We're at the point where we need to do surgery to make sure it doesn't tear,' Luc said. 'And we've got three options, depending on what you'd like to do. May I ask, were you thinking of having children?'

'I'd like to,' Maia said, 'but my partner's worried. Not so much the risks of the baby having Marfan's, because we can have IVF and with preimplantation genetic diagnosis so we can be sure the baby doesn't have the gene, but he read up that women with Marfan's were more at risk of aortic rupture, especially during pregnancy.'

'And he doesn't want to lose you,' Luc said softly. 'I understand that. Surgery now will take that risk away.' He drew three quick pictures. 'The first option is where we replace part of the aorta and its root, including the valve. The treatment's very safe and has a long track record, but you'll be at risk of developing a blood clot so you'll need blood-thinning medication for the rest of your life.'

'Which means I can't get pregnant, right?'

'Which means if you do want to try for a baby, your doctor will switch your blood-thinning meds to one that's injected under the skin and doesn't cross the placenta,' Luc said. 'Or we can do a different sort of surgery where we replace part of the aorta but keep your valve—it's called a valve sparing root replacement or VSRR for short. Because we're keeping your valve, you won't need the blood-thinning medication, but there's a one in four chance we'll have to redo the operation within the next twenty years.'

Maia looked thoughtful. 'What's the third?'

'It's a very new treatment where we make a special sleeve to go round your aorta, called a personalised external aortic root support or PEARS.'

'So it wraps round and acts like a support, say like when my knee's playing up and I have to strap it up?' Maia asked.

'Yes. The idea is that it'll keep your aorta at the size it is now, so it won't get any wider in the future—and that reduces the risk of a tear or the valve leaking. The procedure's not as invasive as replacing the root or the valve-sparing surgery, though I'll still need to open your chest under a general anaesthetic. And it means it'll be more appropriate if you do want to have a baby, because it'll keep your aorta at this size and reduce the risks during pregnancy. But it's still a very new procedure,' Luc warned, 'so not that many have been done.'

'So how do you do it? Wrap it round?'

'We give you a CT scan and we make a 3D computer model of your aorta from the scan, print it, and we use that to make a fabric mesh support tailored exactly to your aorta,' Luc explained.

'3D printing? That sounds cool,' Maia said. 'I know you said it's new, but have you done many?'

'You'll be my second patient—and the first at this hospital,' Luc said. 'Though, if you decide to go for that option, I'll ask one of my former colleagues to come over and assist, because he's got more experience than I have. Or it might be that we end up doing the operation at my old hospital.'

'Can I talk the options over with my husband?' Maia asked.

'Of course,' Luc said. 'I'll want to see you again anyway, and maybe he can come with you if he has any questions. Though I'll give you some leaflets to take away with you—it's a lot to remember and it's always good to have things written down so you can refer back.'

'Thank you,' Maia said. 'I know there are risks, but I'm leaning towards that 3D support thing. I like the sound of that much more.'

'Let's book you in my clinic for next week,' Luc said, 'and you can talk it over with your husband in the meantime and bring all your questions with you to clinic.'

After clinic, he managed to catch Kelly. 'Are you free for lunch? I could do with your opinion on something.'

'Sure.' She smiled at him.

'Maybe we could grab a sandwich and head over to the park,' he suggested. Where it would be quieter and more private than the hospital canteen and he could sound her out.

'That sounds good,' she said.

'Thanks for doing that echo on Maia Isley for me,' he said when they'd found a quiet bench in the park.

'Her aorta's quite a bit bigger than last time. Are you planning surgery?' she asked.

'She's talking it over with her husband, but there's a fairly big chance she'll opt for PEARS.'

'Aortal support?' Her eyes gleamed. 'If she does, I'd love to sit in on the op. I've heard about it but not seen it done.'

'Given that you're her cardiologist,' he said, 'if she takes that option then you'll be involved in the CT scans and you can definitely sit in on the op. We might need to print the 3D model of her heart elsewhere, but I'm sure Sanjay will be happy for you to be involved, and maybe do a presentation to the rest of the team. I need to talk to one of my old colleagues as well as Sanjay, so we might end up doing the actual op at the Royal Hampstead Free instead of here, or it might be that my colleague comes here to help out.'

'I am so up for that,' she said. 'I've never done anything like that before.'

He smiled. 'That's important to you, isn't it? Being able to make a difference.'

'Yes. And I'm pretty sure it's the same for you.'

'It is.' Should he ask her now? He'd been thinking about it ever since Elle had called him. He took a deep breath and said carefully, 'I think you and I could make a difference for each other.'

'Job enrichment? Absolutely,' she agreed. 'We've got a new F1 doctor starting next week. I'm responsible for her training, and it'd be great if she could do some observation or even some work in the operating theatre as well as in the cath lab. And your trainee surgeon might enjoy doing some stent work with us.'

'That's fine, but actually I was thinking on a more personal level.' He paused. 'What you were saying the other week about inventing a boyfriend.'

She frowned. 'What about it?'

'I need to get married. So if you married me, it would solve a problem for both of us.'

Her green eyes widened in apparent shock. 'What? That's crazy!'

He winced. He'd been thinking about this

for a while; for her, this was completely out of the blue. 'Sorry. I could have put that better. I'm not hitting on you, Kelly. I mean a marriage in name only.'

'You're the heir to the kingdom of Bordimiglia,' she said. 'Surely you've got to marry someone of royal blood? And why do you need to get married? And why me?'

It was a fair list of questions. 'This is in confidence, yes?'

'It's a little late to be asking that now,' she said. 'I might be the heart of the hospital gossip machine.'

'I'm pretty sure you're not,' he said, 'though you have a point.'

'OK. In confidence.'

'Trust you, you're a doctor?' he asked wryly.

'You started this,' she reminded him. 'And you haven't given me any answers yet.'

'From the top—my parents expect me to get married to someone who'd be suitable as a queen. So, yes, you're probably right about the royal bloodline. The problem is, someone who wants to be queen doesn't want to be married to a cardiac surgeon.' He knew that from bitter experience. 'A cardiac surgeon is who I am and who I want to be.'

She frowned. 'But you're a prince. Don't you have to take over from your dad?'

'Technically, yes. But he's the king and he can change the rules of succession if he wants to,' Luc explained. 'I told you I have two sisters, Eleonora and Giulia. Elle's the oldest and she'd make an absolutely brilliant queen. Apart from the fact that she's good with people and everyone loves her, she's astute—she's got a real business mind, and she'd do a lot for our country.'

'Would she actually want the job, though?' Kelly asked.

'We've talked about it, and she agrees that she'd make a better ruler than I would. She already does a lot of royal duties and she advises our father on ecology issues. I don't believe I should get the job just because I'm the son. And I'm a much better doctor than I am a politician. I know I've had a really privileged life and I appreciate that. I'm not shirking my duty—I want to serve my country in a different way, to make it a leading research centre for cardiac health. In a couple of years' time, I want to go back to Bordimiglia with everything I've learned here and set up a new cardiac centre. All our father has to do is change the rules of succession, so then his oldest child instead of his son will take over when he decides to step down. Elle deserves her chance to change our bit of the world. All I'm suggesting is pushing a little bit harder to give her that chance.'

'So getting married to someone who doesn't have royal blood will make you ineligible to rule?' Kelly asked.

'Technically, no, but getting married to a fellow doctor would give my parents a very clear signal that I'm committed to my life as a cardiac surgeon.' Given that she was a work-aholic—and he knew exactly why—maybe there was something else he could offer to sweeten the deal. 'I'm going to need good staff when I set up that cardiac centre, including someone who could help to train the cardi-ologists of the future.' He paused. 'I'd like to headhunt you.'

'Me.' She looked thoughtful.

'I want to change people's lives for the bet-ter,' Luc said.

'As a surgeon, you do that on a one-to-one basis. As a king, you could do that for a lot more people, all at the same time,' she pointed out.

'Except I don't actually want to be a king,' he said. 'I love my job and I don't want to give it up. As I said, I'm not shirking my duty—Elle would make a better ruler than I ever could. It's in everyone's best interests for her to be the next ruler.'

'I'm not sure getting married will convince your parents of anything,' she said. 'And I really don't get why you're asking me.'

'Because you're a fellow doctor. You understand my working hours and you don't have any false expectations about my life as a surgeon,' he said. 'And it will help you out, because if you're married then your family and friends won't need to keep trying to find you a suitable partner.'

Kelly stared at Luc.

He seemed perfectly serious.

She couldn't quite get her head round this. The heir to the throne of Bordimiglia had just suggested that they get married—offering her a marriage of convenience that would stop everyone trying to find her a new partner and make his parents realise that he wanted to keep his career as a surgeon. It was the last thing she'd expected. OK, so she'd said to him that she'd been tempted to invent a boyfriend to get her family and friends to back off from the matchmaking: but there was a huge difference between an imaginary boyfriend and a marriage of convenience.

'We've known each other for less than a month,' she said. 'I admit, I looked you up on the Internet before you started here so I know a lot about you—but you know next to nothing about me. For all you know, I could be an axe-murderer.'

To his credit, he blushed slightly. 'You're not.'

Then she realised what he must've done. 'You had me checked out?'

'Yes,' he admitted, 'though I was pretty sure before that. You wouldn't have spent all these years training as a cardiologist if you were an axe-murderer. Plus I've worked with you. Anyone who works with you will know exactly who you are—you're caring, you're bright and you're very good at your job.'

It wasn't often Kelly was lost for words, but she'd never had a near-stranger propose marriage to her before. And this was so out of the blue. Getting married was a huge thing. How could he sound so casual about it?

'The way I see it,' he continued, 'we're in a similar situation and we can help each other.'

'We're not at all in a similar situation,' she countered.

'But the same solution would work for both of us,' he said.

'I—we—I can't get married to you, Luc,' she said. 'What about love?'

'We don't need it. This would be a marriage in name only. We're giving each other a breathing space from other people who want us to do things we don't want to do.'

'What if one of us falls in love with someone?'

'Then we'll have a quiet divorce,' he said.

A really nasty thought struck her. 'Is that your price for putting Jake and Summer on your trial?'

'No, that's totally separate and it depends on whether or not their doctor approves. I'm still waiting to hear back. If their doctor says no, I'll still do whatever I can to help them, but I'll need to see their medical history before I can make any kind of suggestions.'

Which was fair enough. You had to know the facts about your patient before you could suggest a course of treatment. 'Marriage.' She shook her head. 'I married Simon because I loved him. Getting married to you, when we barely know each other, and for such a cynical reason—that seems wrong.'

'Don't say no just yet,' he said. 'Take some time to think about it. What I'm suggesting is a marriage in name only. I'll make no demands on you. And we can give it a time limit—six months. That should give you enough time for your family and friends to back off and let you move on when you're ready, and for me to convince my father to do the right thing and make Elle his official heir.'

'Six months,' she repeated. 'And then what?'

'A quiet separation and eventual divorce,' he said. 'Though if you want to come back with me to Bordimiglia and help to train the cardiologists, then we can stay married for longer. Whatever suits you best.'

Being involved in a cutting-edge cardiac facility and training the cardiologists of the future... In a different country. A brand-new opportunity to save lives and a complete change in her own life.

Maybe this was what she needed to help her finally move on from the past. A new start.

'So what exactly would this marriage entail?' she asked.

'You'd need to live with me, to make it look convincing,' he said. 'But my place is big enough for you to have your own room. Your own suite, if that's what you'd prefer.'

She couldn't quite get her head round this offer.

'Please, just think about it,' he said, clearly thinking that she was going to refuse. 'I need your help, and in return I can help you. Talk it over with someone you trust.'

'Won't you have to vet them, first?'

'If you trust them, that's good enough for

me,' he said softly. 'Talk it over. Then you and I can revisit it—say a week today.'

She was pretty sure her answer would still be the same in a week's time. But he'd asked for her help, and it felt mean to refuse without even thinking about it. That wasn't who she was. Talking it over with her sister would be impossible; if she was going to convince Susie to stop trying to fix her up with someone, telling her about Luc's marriage of convenience idea would make Susie even more worried. But maybe her best friend would be a good sounding board—and Angela was supersensible. She might come up with a better solution to both their problems.

Kelly saw a lot of Luc over the next couple of days. She ended up having lunch with him on Friday, but he didn't push her to give him an early answer. Instead, he made her laugh, telling her tales from his student days, and about one of his uncles who'd told him and his sisters spooky stories and then hidden inside a suit of armour in the castle and scared them all by making them think the suit of armour was a ghost walking.

The more time she spent with him, the more she found herself having fun—something she hadn't really done since Simon's death. Maybe

Luc was the one who could help her move on. She could help him and he could help her.

Though she had a feeling that he hadn't told her the whole story. He'd made that comment about her being a fellow doctor who could understand the hours he worked. Had his parents expected him to date someone with the right background but who hadn't appreciated that Luc was dedicated to his career—someone who had hurt him, perhaps?

She'd have to think of a tactful way to ask him.

And in the meantime she'd planned to see her best friend for dinner.

She made Angela's favourite, sweet potato and black bean curry for dinner on Saturday night. But Angela almost choked on it when Kelly told her about Luc's suggestion.

'Have you lost your mind?' Angela asked. 'The hospital clinic thing, yes—that'd probably do you a lot of good, giving you a fresh start. But marrying someone you barely know? Of all the insane schemes...'

'I'd been thinking about inventing a boyfriend so everyone would back off. And this would do the same thing. If I was married, Susie would stop trying to find me a partner, so would Mum and so would y—' Kelly stopped. 'Um.'

'So would I?' Angela frowned. 'It's been two years, Kel. Simon loved you and he wouldn't—'

'—have wanted me to be alone,' Kelly finished. 'I know. Ange, we've been through all this. I haven't met anyone who's made me feel in the slightest bit how I felt about Simon.' She ignored her growing awareness of Luc. That wasn't the same thing at all.

'You weren't madly in love with Simon from the very first second you met him. Your feelings for each other developed as you got to know each other. So you're not comparing apples with apples, are you?' Angela asked. 'You have to give someone a chance to grow on you.'

'Actually, Simon and I knew pretty early on. And I'm really, *really* tired of being paraded in front of suitable men,' Kelly said.

'Technically, I think the men are being paraded in front of you,' Angela pointed out.

'You know what I mean. Getting married would stop the matchmaking.'

'But why did he ask *you*?'

'Because we're in a similar situation.' She gave her best friend a wry smile. 'Funny, he said that to me, and I disagreed—but the more I've thought about it, the more I realise that he's right. Getting married would solve both our problems.'

'You can't get married to someone you don't love and who doesn't love you. And he's a *prince*, Kel. You'll have the media on your back for the rest of your life.'

'I haven't got a wild past,' Kelly said. 'So it's not an issue. I'm boring.'

'Of course you're not boring.'

'In terms of front-page news, I am.'

Angela frowned. 'OK. Just supposing you do go along with this, what about his family?'

'He thinks this will convince his parents that his older sister—who actually wants to do the job—would be a better ruler than he is.'

'Hmm.' Angela didn't look convinced. 'I foresee lots of arguing, and because they're who they are it'll all be in public. Tell him he's crazy.' Her eyes narrowed. 'Or is there something you're not telling me? Are you already dating him?'

'I work with him. He's nice with junior staff, he's brilliant with patients and watching him work is amazing. I'm getting the chance to do cutting edge stuff.'

Angela looked thoughtful. 'You haven't denied that you're dating him.'

'He's my colleague.'

Angela scoffed. 'You marrying a stranger—'

'Marrying a colleague, in name only,' Kelly corrected.

'But someone you've known for just a few short weeks.'

'Almost a month,' Kelly pointed out.

'That's the definition of a stranger in anyone's books. Nobody's going to believe it.'

Kelly frowned. 'So people will think I'm a gold-digger?'

'Anyone who knows you will know that's not true,' Angela said. 'No, I mean nobody will believe you're marrying someone you barely know. You loved Simon. No way will you settle for anything less than love.'

'It could be a whirlwind romance,' Kelly said thoughtfully.

Angela blinked. 'So *that's* what you're not telling me. You like him. And I don't mean just as a colleague.'

Kelly felt the colour rise in her face. 'That isn't the deal. It's a marriage in name only.'

'So you *do* like him.'

Kelly squirmed. 'It feels wrong. It feels disloyal to Simon. And, anyway, Luc doesn't feel like that about me.'

'But he asked you to marry him.'

'To solve a problem for both of us and give us both breathing space.'

'If he wanted to convince his parents that he's unsuitable for the job, surely he should marry someone completely unsuitable—say the modern equivalent of a Wallis Simpson?' Angela suggested.

'He's trying to convince them that he wants to keep doing what he's already spent his life either training for or actually doing. Marrying a fellow doctor kind of underlines that.'

Angela groaned. 'You're talking yourself into this.'

Kelly shook her head. 'Right now, I'm asking your advice.'

'That's easy. Don't get married,' Angela said promptly. 'Surely dating him will be enough?'

'For me, it would,' Kelly said. 'But not for him.'

'Kel, you got married to Simon because you loved him. How can you even think about getting married for any other reason this time?'

'We're helping each other out.'

'It's insane.'

'You could,' Kelly suggested, 'meet him for yourself and see what you think.'

'It sounds as if you've already made your mind up,' Angela said.

'He's not pushing me for an immediate answer. He said I should talk it over with someone I trust. Which is you.'

'I love you, Kel,' Angela said. 'You've been my best friend since we met on the first day of sixth form. But I worry that if you do this you're going to get hurt. You've already been through enough, losing Simon.'

'Did I say Luc's doing a trial for HCM patients? There's a possibility that Jake and Summer could be on it.'

Angela's eyes widened. 'I hope that this marriage thing isn't a condition for them being on the trial.'

'Of course it isn't. I don't think it's a condition of the job offer and I'd love the chance to be involved in training the cardiologists of the future. What I'm trying to say is that he's not going to hurt me,' Kelly explained. 'He's one of the good guys. We're just doing each other a favour.'

'An insane favour,' Angela said, and hugged her. 'Think about it a bit more. Do yourself a list of pros and cons so you can make a really informed decision. But, whatever you do, don't rush into it. Because I think this could go very wrong, very quickly.'

CHAPTER FOUR

KELLY THOUGHT ABOUT it all weekend. Was Angela right and it would all end in tears? Or would it work the way Luc thought it would, and buy them both some time?

On Monday, she was still undecided.

'Can we talk over lunch?' Luc asked when he saw her in the staff kitchen before their shift started.

'How about over dinner tonight?' she suggested. 'My place? It'll be more private than the hospital canteen.'

'That'd be good. What time?' he asked.

'Half past seven?'

'OK. Let me know the address,' he said.

'I'll text you,' she promised. 'Let me know if there's anything you don't eat or you have any allergies.'

'No allergies and I eat anything,' he said. 'I'll bring the wine—red or white?'

'You really don't need to.'

'Red or white?' he repeated.

She smiled. 'White. Thank you.'

Offering to cook dinner for a prince. Was she crazy? He must be used to eating meals cooked by Michelin-starred chefs. Then again, she knew he saw himself as a surgeon rather than a prince, so maybe this was more like cooking dinner for a colleague. A friend. *A potential husband in name only…*

She pushed the thought out of her mind and concentrated on her clinic and her ward round. After her shift was over, she headed for the supermarket and bought salmon, Puy lentils, Chantenay carrots, spinach, fresh ginger and a lime. She knew she already had mixed berries and Greek yoghurt in her fridge; she bought a box of shortbread thins to go with them, then headed back to her flat to marinade the salmon.

At half past seven precisely, her doorbell rang. Luc stood on the doorstep, carrying a beautiful bouquet of flowers and a bottle of wine.

'Thank you. They're lovely, but you really didn't have to,' she said, accepting the flowers and the wine.

'I wanted to,' he said.

'And this wine is from Bordimiglia?' she asked, looking at the label.

'It's a white Pinot Noir—and it's very drinkable,' he said with a smile. 'It's from one of the vineyards on our estate.'

But his parents didn't just own a vineyard. They ruled the country.

'Do you need a temporary parking permit for your car, or did you get a taxi?' she asked.

'A permit would be great—my driver's staying with the car.'

Driver? Of course. He'd need to have someone on security detail. She had to remind herself that Luc was a prince first and a doctor second, even if he saw himself as being the other way round. 'I'm so sorry. I didn't think to make dinner for your driver. I can add a few more veg and make it stretch a bit.'

'It's fine. He's got a sandwich and a bottle of water.'

'Even so, if he'd like to join us, he's more than welcome. Ask him when you take the permit out.' She took a permit from the kitchen drawer, scratched off the date and time and handed it to Luc.

When Luc came back, he said, 'Gino says thank you for the offer, but he's happy with his sandwich.'

But she still felt like a terrible hostess. 'At the very least I can make the poor man a cup of coffee.'

'He won't say no to that. Black, no sugar,' Luc said. 'And yes, I do make coffee for my security team. I don't expect them to wait on me.'

But they were always there. Even though they were discreet, they were always there. He never had time on his own. 'It must be hard, living your life in public all the time.'

Luc shrugged. 'I was born into it, so I've never known anything different. I guess it'd be harder if you don't come from that kind of background.'

'Is that what happened?' she asked gently. 'You met someone, but they couldn't cope with being in a goldfish bowl?'

'Something like that.' For a second, he looked really sad. 'There are two sides to my life—Luc Bianchi, the cardiac surgeon, and Prince Luciano, heir to the kingdom of Bordimiglia. I'm pretty much stuck in the middle. Women who embrace Prince Luciano's lifestyle don't like the other side of me, or the hours I work; and women who date Luc the surgeon don't tend to like the Bordimiglia side.' He spread his hands. 'Until everything is resolved with my father, I can't really be clear about who I am and what my partner can expect from life—and it's unfair to get involved with someone who wants one side of me and might well end up with the other instead.'

'Hence your insa—' She bit back the word, and instead said, 'idea of getting married.' She made coffee and opened the box of shortbread thins. 'Take some of these to Gino to go with the coffee.'

'I will.' He smiled at her. 'You're a kind woman, Kelly.'

She brushed aside the compliment. 'It's what any normal person would do.'

His expression said otherwise, but he took the coffee and biscuits out to Gino. 'Something smells good,' he said when he came back.

'Baked salmon marinated in ginger and lime, on a bed of Puy lentils, with steamed Chantenay carrots and spinach,' she told him.

He grinned. 'I don't think you can get any more heart-healthy than that. Then again, given that you're a cardiologist...'

'Oh, I practise what I preach,' she said, smiling. 'I'm not telling my patients to eat a Mediterranean diet while I tuck into masses of high-fat, low-fibre junk. But I also don't think that eating healthily has to be boring.'

'Agreed.' He paused. 'Can I do anything?'

'Open the wine, if you like. I'm about to serve up.'

He did so, and they sat at the small bistro table next to the French doors that overlooked her patio.

'This is lovely,' he said after his first mouthful.

She smiled. 'Pleasure.'

'It's a nice flat,' he said.

'Thanks. It's within walking distance of the hospital, too.'

'Did you live here with your husband?'

She shook her head. 'I moved here a year ago. I had a lot of happy memories in our old flat, but it made me sad to go home. I stuck it out for a year—people say it's not a good idea to make big changes until a year after the funeral—and then I found this place.'

'I can see why you like it.' He gestured to the garden. 'And you get the sun here in the evening. That's always nice.'

But he wasn't here to make small talk. She took a gulp of the wine to give her courage. 'Oh. That's very nice.' She took a deep breath. 'I guess we need to discuss your, um, proposal.'

'Did you talk to anyone about it?'

She nodded. 'My best friend, Angela. She's an accountant and she's very sensible.'

'And?'

'She thinks it's…' She paused, thinking of

a tactful way to say it. 'She thinks the job in the new clinic would be good for me, but the marriage bit isn't workable.'

'Why?'

'Because I married Simon for love, and she thinks I wouldn't settle for anything less, second time round. You're practically a stranger.'

'Fair point,' he said.

'So I was thinking. My original idea was to have a fake boyfriend. Maybe I can be your fake girlfriend instead,' she suggested.

'Fake dating would work for your situation,' he said, 'but it wouldn't be enough to convince my parents that I'm a surgeon rather than a prince.'

'A fake engagement, then,' Kelly said.

He shook his head. 'Engagements can be broken off. It's got to be marriage.'

'It's not plausible, Luc,' she said. 'We've known each other for a little less than a month. Yes, we get on well at work and as part of the team outside work, and I think we're well on the way to becoming friends—I like you and I think you like me.'

'Agreed.'

She ignored the little shiver of desire that rippled down her spine. That wasn't appropriate. They were talking about liking each other, not attraction. 'But you're a prince. You can't get married just like that.' She snapped her fingers. 'I mean no offence and I'm certainly not saying you're unlovable, but nobody is going to believe that I'd get married to you. Work with you, yes, and come and help you set up the clinic—but not married.'

'What if,' he said, 'we had a whirlwind romance?'

'That's what I said to Angela.' She wrinkled her nose. 'OK. Supposing we pretend to start dating and get everyone to believe we've fallen madly in love with each other within the space of a couple of weeks. That's just about plausible. But I still don't think anyone would believe that either of us would rush into marriage. I'm thirty-two and you're…?'

'Thirty-five,' he confirmed.

'Exactly. We're not impulsive teenagers, Luc. We're old enough to be sensible. We both have responsible jobs—positions that take years of training and experience. We're not going to get married in a rush.'

'Maybe we've had this whirlwind romance, I whisked you off to New York for a mini break and we got so carried away by the romance of the city that we applied for a wedding licence while we were out there,' he suggested.

She frowned. 'Surely you have to apply for a wedding licence weeks in advance?'

'In New York, you can get married twenty-four hours after you get the permit,' he said.

She looked at him. 'You've researched it, haven't you?'

'Yes,' he admitted. 'And it would work. We could fly to New York for a midweek break. We'd apply for our licence on our first day there, have dinner somewhere fancy and catch a show on Broadway maybe, then get married the second day.'

'You mean we'd elope?' But her family and friends would be so hurt if she got married again without any of them being there. Though if she told them the truth, that it was a marriage of convenience to help Luc, that would make the whole thing pointless regarding her own situation.

'Eloping stops all the complications,' he said.

Not in her eyes. 'Won't your family and friends be hurt that you didn't want to share your special day with them?' she asked.

'They'd understand that you, as a widow, would want this to be low-key.' He wrinkled his nose. 'The alternative would be a full-blown State wedding in Bordimiglia.'

That was definitely out of the question. 'Sorry. I can't stand in a church and make promises, not when I've...' The words stuck

in her throat. Not when she'd done it before.
For love.

He reached across the table and squeezed
her hand briefly. 'I'm sorry. I'm being selfish
and asking too much. It's something I've been
thinking about for a while, and what pushed
me into asking you is that my sister Elle rang
me last weekend. She told me that our father
wants to retire within the next year. Which
means I'm running out of options. I need to
act now.'

'I still don't see how getting married will
make your parents think that you're not fit to
be king,' Kelly said.

'Not that I'm unfit to be king,' he corrected,
'but that I'm committed to a life in medicine.
Getting married to a doctor in a related spe-
cialty could do that.'

'Can't you just talk to your parents?' she
asked.

'I've tried, believe me. I've brought it up
time and time again. But my father's stubborn,' he said wryly.

'Getting married won't change things,' she
said. 'Why don't we brainstorm other ways to
help you stay as a surgeon?'

He spread his hands. 'I'm all ears.'

She thought about it. And thought some
more. 'I've drawn a blank,' she was forced to

admit in the end. 'I know if I told my parents what I wanted to do, they'd tell me to follow my dreams and they would support me. But I think it's different for you. There are expectations.'

'Exactly. But I understand why it's not an option for you.'

Just for a moment, his expression was so bleak and lonely. Her heart went out to him. She'd been there; she knew how it felt, with loneliness like a black hole sucking you in. This time, she was the one to reach across the table and squeeze his hand. 'I can't believe nobody's fallen in love with you before—or that you haven't fallen for someone.'

'Things don't always work out the way you plan,' he said.

'What happened?' Then she grimaced. 'Sorry, that was unspeakably nosy of me. Ignore that. You don't have to answer.'

'No. I've dragged you in this far. You deserve the truth. I did fall in love with someone, when I was in my last year as a medical student. I thought Rachel loved me.' He blew out a breath. 'I met her family and we got on well. So then I took her back to Bordimiglia to meet mine. They liked her. She seemed to like them, too.'

So what had been the problem? Kelly wondered.

'But she was really quiet on the way back to London. And she didn't ask me to stay over at her place, that night, the way she usually did.' He looked away. 'She wasn't in lectures, the next day, and she didn't answer her phone. I was worried about her, so I called round. And that's when she broke up with me. She said she loved me, but she couldn't handle the public side of my life—seeing speculation in the news about her, having her dad's speeding fine dragged up and her sister's divorce spread across the gossip pages. She'd been doorstepped that morning by a couple of paps—it must've been a slow news week and they'd picked up on me taking her to meet my family, then dug up every single bit of dirt they could while we were away. I'd gone straight into lectures so I hadn't seen the papers.' He sighed. 'If I'd been just a normal medical student, it would have been fine. Rachel and I would have been married by now, maybe with a couple of children if we were lucky.'

'But you're a prince,' she said softly.

He nodded. 'The same thing happened with the next two women I dated who weren't from the same kind of background as me. They were fine with me working the stupid hours of a junior doctor, because they did it themselves. But they hated the protocol and politics of the other side of my life—not to mention the press intrusion.'

'What about dating someone from your background?'

He shrugged. 'I tried that, too. They were fine with the protocols and the formality and the dressing up.'

'But they weren't so keen on dating a doctor?' Kelly guessed.

'Not when they missed a film premiere because I was stuck in the operating theatre, or I got called away from a dinner party because a patient had developed complications and I needed to be there. I mean—did they seriously expect me to walk away from my patient in the middle of an op and tell the head of department to find someone else to finish the operation because I had to go to a *party*?' For a moment, he looked disgusted. 'I guess the answer is for me to give up my job and do what my father wants.'

'But you'd be miserable and all the experience you have would be wasted. You're bringing new procedures to our department, things that will make a real difference,' she said. 'You're helping to train the surgeons of the future.'

'Which would be the whole point of my clinic in Bordimiglia. Cutting-edge stuff.'

'That's not the same as being a whiny, over-indulged brat who's rebelling against what his parents want just for the sake of it,' she said.

'Thank you for understanding.' He looked sad. 'I can't see a way out. If I stay as I am, it's going to upset my parents—they'll feel I'm rejecting them. If I give up my career as a surgeon, I feel as if I'm throwing away all the help I've been given from my tutors and my colleagues over the years, not to mention letting my patients down. And yes, sure, as the king I could still set up a new hospital—but I wouldn't be the one working there and making a difference and passing on my skills to younger surgeons. And what's the point if I'm not going to be involved with patients? I want my skills to make a difference, not my finance.' He shrugged. 'Whatever I do, I lose.'

'Whereas if it's your father's idea to change the rules of succession...'

'Then that would make me fourth in line for the throne, behind Elle and my nephew Alessio and niece Anna. Which is perfect.'

She bit her lip. 'I'd like to help you. But getting married—that's a huge step.'

'I know I'm asking a lot. And we don't know each other very well. And, really, what do you get out of marrying me? A massive disruption to your life.'

'According to my family and friends, I don't have a life—just work,' she said.

'I'd be the same, in your shoes,' he said. 'I'd want to double-check everything so no patient ever went undiagnosed again. Which isn't possible, because if someone doesn't show any symptoms they wouldn't have any reason to get themselves checked out, and you wouldn't get the chance to diagnose them.'

'I know. My head agrees with you,' she said.

'But your heart doesn't?'

'No,' she admitted. 'And I think that's partly why I can't move on. Because I still think I should've noticed something.'

'Nobody could've noticed it,' he said. 'But you got his brother and his niece checked out.'

'It doesn't feel like enough,' she said. She blew out a breath. 'I can't fix my situation, but I guess I could help you fix yours.'

'Which isn't a fair exchange. It feels as if I'm using you,' he said, 'and that's not who I am.'

'You're not using me, because you're not making any false promises. You're offering me an opportunity with the job, a chance to make a real difference and have a fresh start. Something to look forward to instead of backwards. And you have a point that everyone will stop nagging me to date if I'm married.' She looked at him. 'I love my family and friends, and they'd expect to be invited to my wedding.'

'Which means mine would need to be there, and then it'd be a complete circus.'

Kelly noticed that Luc hadn't said anything about loving his family. Or maybe it was different, in royal circles, and duty took precedence over love.

'It's possible to arrange a quick State wedding,' he said, 'but then the media would be all over it, speculating that you were pregnant, and...' He grimaced. 'It'd be easier if we eloped.'

'I can't do that. It'd hurt everyone and make them feel pushed away, and they've all been so supportive. I can't get married in a rush to someone they've never even met.'

'What if it was a whirlwind romance and I swept you off your feet?'

'Prince Charming?' she asked wryly.

He narrowed his eyes at her. 'Not funny.'

'Sorry.'

He wrinkled his nose. 'Actually, I should be the one apologising for the sense of humour failure. If it wasn't so close to home, it would actually be funny.'

'Apology accepted,' she said.

'I know I'm asking a lot,' he said. 'But I could make it worth—'

'Don't you dare insult me by offering me any kind of payment,' she warned, before he could offer.

'How about I make a donation to a charity of your choice?' he suggested, and named a substantial amount of money.

She felt her eyes widen. 'Luc, that's a small fortune.'

'It's worth it to me,' he said softly. 'It means I can follow my dreams and I'm free to be who I really am.'

'I want to help you, Luc. But marriage is huge.'

'I know.' He paused. 'Don't say no just yet. Let's spend a few days getting to know each other better. And then, if you feel we can go ahead, I can maybe meet your family and convince them I'm sweeping you off your feet.' He gave her a wry smile. 'Though this feels a bit like that film my sisters loved, the one with the woman who's about to be deported so she proposes to her secretary.'

'Oh, the one with Sandra Bullock and Ryan Reynolds? I loved that.' She smiled. 'Or the

Gerard Depardieu one, where he and Andie MacDowell made that whole fake photo album so he could get his green card, and he got deported.'

'Except we're going to carry this off and not get found out.'

'Problem is, I've already talked to my best friend about it. Not that Ange would say anything if I ask her not to. She's just worried that I'm going to get hurt.'

'I promise you're not going to get hurt, and I can make exactly the same promise to her,' Luc said. 'I keep my promises.'

'That's good to know.'

'And your dad doesn't have a speeding conviction and your sister's happily married, so there will be no nasty headlines about anyone in your family.'

She winced. 'So you know about my whole family from your dossier on me?'

'It's not that big a dossier. Just enough to establish the basics, and confirm that the press won't be able to drag up anything to pillory you with,' he said. 'But you're right. We need to get to know each other. So. You always wanted to be a doctor?'

'When I was really little, I wanted to be a ballerina, like in the Angelina stories. Except I was truly hopeless at classes and always fell over my feet. And then I thought I might like to be a gardener, like my grandad, and grow beautiful flowers. And then one of my teachers suggested being a doctor, and I liked the thought of being able to make a difference. So I did the three sciences for my A-Levels, got into uni and ended up training here.' She smiled at him. 'I know you said you wanted to become a doctor after your best friend died.'

'Specifically a cardiologist. Except when I worked in the cardiac department I discovered that I liked surgery. Though I did flirt a bit with being in a rock band,' he confessed. 'I was the rhythm guitarist and did the backing vocals in a band called Prince of Hearts when I was a student.'

She laughed. 'That's such a perfect name. Did you write your own stuff?'

He smiled back. 'No. And if I'm honest we weren't much good. It was fun, though.'

'There's a band in the hospital—Maybe Baby,' she said. 'Half of them are in the maternity ward and half in paediatrics. They play all the hospital functions. You never know— you could join them.'

'I'm *really* not that good,' he said. 'And I can prove that to you if you'd like to have dinner at my place on Wednesday.'

'You're on.' She looked at him. 'So do you do the cooking, or do you have staff?'

He winced. 'A mix of the two. It's not because I'm too spoiled to cook.'

'You're a cardiac surgeon. You work long hours. If you lived on your own, it'd be takeaways or microwave meals.'

'Is that what you do?' he asked.

'No. But I like cooking.' She paused. 'I'm assuming your security staff live in, so your place is a lot bigger than this.'

'Yes,' he said. 'But I will cook for you myself on Wednesday. Is there anything you hate, or are allergic to?'

'I don't eat red meat, but other than that I'm easy to cook for,' she said with a smile.

'I'd also like to take you out tomorrow night, if you're free?' he asked. 'To a restaurant,' he clarified, 'then I can have all my focus on you and not on burning your dinner.'

She laughed and nodded. 'That would be lovely.'

He lifted his glass. 'Here's to getting to know each other better.'

Kelly echoed the toast. But part of her was wondering just what she'd let herself in for.

CHAPTER FIVE

On Tuesday, Kelly and Luc were both busy with patients and Kelly's morning overran when she was called down to the emergency department to see a six-year-old girl who'd had a cardiac arrest. Jordan's mum had died from Long QT Syndrome, a condition that caused an electrical disturbance to the heart which could lead to a dangerous heart rhythm. The condition could be inherited—like Simon's hypertrophic cardiomyopathy—and, according to the notes, Jordan had had a previous cardiac arrest on the way home from school, two years before. Thankfully Jordan's grandmother had learned emergency life skills at work and had been able to resuscitate her.

'So the doctors didn't suggest fitting an ICD, last time?' Kelly asked Mrs Martin, Jordan's grandmother, out of earshot of the little girl while Jordan's grandfather stayed by her bedside.

Mrs Martin shook her head. 'They said the medication would be enough.'

Medication was the first-line treatment for the condition, but Kelly would've scheduled in frequent cardio tests if the girl had been her patient. 'OK. Did they explain Long QT Syndrome to you?'

'Not really.' Mrs Martin grimaced. 'I read up about it and, when we moved to London, I asked our family doctor if he thought Jordan might need an operation. He said the medication was working so leave it for now.'

'As you've read up about the condition, you know that Jordan's at risk of having more cardiac arrests.'

'And she could die suddenly, like Savannah did.'

'Yes,' Kelly admitted. 'It's brave of you to say it out loud.'

'I don't feel very brave,' Mrs Martin admitted. 'I'm terrified we're going to lose her.'

'There is an option that will help,' Kelly said. 'You might have read about it. It's an ICD—that stands for "implantable cardiac defibrillator"—and it's a little device about the size of a matchbox. If Jordan's heart rhythm suddenly becomes abnormal, the ICD will give her heart a tiny electric shock and that will make her heart go back into the right rhythm.'

'So it means an operation?'

'Yes. I can do it here in the cath lab. For adults, I'd do it under a local anaesthetic with sedation, so they'd be too sleepy to remember anything. But, because Jordan's so young, I'd rather do this under a general anaesthetic. You can be with her all the time until she's asleep,' Kelly reassured her, 'and then we'll ask you to wait outside while we do the op, to help us prevent any infection.'

'How long does it take?' Mrs Martin asked.

'A couple of hours,' Kelly said. 'What I'll do is make a small cut here—' she indicated a place below her own collarbone '—to make a little pocket for the ICD. Then I'll connect the electrode to her heart, through a vein, connect the other end of the ICD, test it to make sure it's working, then sew up the cut I made. The stitches will dissolve, so you don't have to worry about them being removed.' She smiled. 'Then we'll wake her up, and you can join her in the recovery area. When she's properly awake, we'll take her back to the children's ward, and she can go home in a couple of days.'

'I...' Mrs Martin swallowed. 'It was hard

enough, losing her mum. I can't lose her as well.'

Kelly took her hand. 'The ICD is going to make things a lot less stressful for both of you. If her heart goes into an abnormal rhythm, the ICD will act like a pacemaker and give her a small electrical signal to make her heart go back to beating normally. If that isn't quite enough, then it will give her a small electric shock and that'll do the trick.'

'And you'll do the operation yourself? We won't have to see another doctor?'

'If there's a complication, I might need to get one of the cardiac surgeons in to give me a hand to fit a slightly different sort of ICD,' Kelly said, 'but in any case I'll be there. Let's go and see Jordan and her grandad, and I'll explain to her what's going to happen and answer any questions you all might have.'

'I just don't want to lose her.' A tear slid down Mrs Martin's cheek. 'It'd be like losing Savannah all over again.'

'Fitting the ICD will give her a much better chance,' Kelly promised. 'While you go and see Jordan and your husband, I'll grab a computer and check the schedule so I can give you a date.'

By the time she'd finished explaining the operation and reassuring Jordan and her grandparents, Kelly had just enough time to grab a sandwich and gulp down a mug of coffee deliberately made half with cold water before her next clinic started. She didn't even bump into Luc on the ward rounds, but he'd left her a text. Pick you up at quarter to seven.

OK, she texted back. Dress code?

Smartish came the answer.

Was she going out with the Prince or with the heart surgeon?

He hadn't said she needed to wear anything as formal as a ballgown, so she hoped that her little black dress would be smart enough, teamed with heels she could also walk in. As it was a nice evening, a walk after dinner would be lovely.

At quarter to seven precisely, he rang her doorbell.

She'd never seen him wear a formal suit before; it looked good on him, and her mouth went dry.

Then she remembered that this wasn't a real date. It was a getting-to-know-you thing to help her decide if she could go ahead with the marriage of convenience. They weren't really going to have a whirlwind courtship. She needed to squash the inappropriate feelings right now.

'You look lovely,' he said.

'Thank you. So do you,' Kelly said, feeling slightly awkward and shy,

He introduced her to Gino, his driver and security detail, and then Gino drove them to a seriously plush hotel overlooking Kensington Park Gardens. 'I thought maybe we could walk through the Italian gardens here, and then along the bank of the Serpentine,' Luc said.

'That sounds perfect,' she said. 'Am I dressed up quite enough for this place, though?'

'You're fine,' he said with a smile.

The menu was amazing. 'It's really hard to choose,' she said.

'The food's good here,' he said. 'I think anything you choose will be excellent.'

And it was also expensive enough not to have prices on the menu.

'We're going halves on the bill,' she said.

'No. My idea, my bill,' he said. 'Don't argue.'

'Provided I can treat you to dinner another time.' She narrowed her eyes at him. 'Assuming I'm fake-dating a heart surgeon.'

His smile was slightly weary. 'You are. And thank you.'

Once they'd chosen their meals, Luc said, 'So tell me about you.'

'I thought you had a dossier on me?'

'Which isn't the same thing at all,' he said. 'It's bare bones.'

'OK. I'm the youngest of two girls. My sister Susie is a lawyer and had twin boys, my dad Robin works in financial services, and so does my mum Caroline. I trained as a doctor in London and I love my job.' She looked at him. 'You?'

'I thought you said you'd looked me up on the Internet?'

'And it's a good rule of thumb not to believe everything you see there,' she pointed out.

He inclined his head. 'Well as I mentioned, I'm the middle of three—my older sister Elle has a girl and a boy, and my younger sister Giulia is married but doesn't have children yet,' he said. 'You know who my parents are. They all work in the family business. I trained in London and stayed because I like the city and I love my job.'

'OK. That's background done,' she said. 'We already know how each other ended up in cardiac medicine. How about music?' she suggested. 'I know you were in a band, so what do you listen to?'

'I operate to Bach because it's regular and calming, but it's nineties indie bands all the way in the gym and when I'm driving,' he said. 'You?'

'My guilty pleasure is eighties pop—the sort of thing I grew up with my mum playing in the kitchen,' she said. 'And I love the Proms. Anything Mozart.' She looked at him. 'Are you actually allowed to go to a gig or a concert?'

He laughed. 'My life isn't *quite* that restricted. Yes. So we can go to some, if you like.'

'That sounds good.' She smiled. 'Movies?'

'Sci-fi and action all the way,' he said.

'How clichéd.' She rolled her eyes. 'Blokey stuff. And there was me hoping that you liked obscure French films.'

'I think that's a double bluff and what you really like seeing are rom-coms—the soppier, the better,' he said.

She laughed. 'Busted. Anything with Ryan Gosling or Tom Hanks is just fine by me. I normally go with Susie or Ange. And I read practically everything.'

'Anything set in Ancient Rome, for me,' he said.

Funny, this was so easy, Kelly thought. Luc was good company, and they had a fair amount in common. This was starting to feel like a proper date, getting to know each other—which was weird and yet nice at the same time. 'So you were saying about music at the gym. I take it you have a personal trainer come to you?'

'I have a gym at home,' he said, 'and a pool. Not just for me—my team use it as well. And sometimes we train together. How about you?

'Dance aerobics a couple of times a week, and taking the boys to the park with Susie at weekends. On wet days, we've taken them to the trampoline park to burn off some energy. They've got this amazing obstacle course that adults can go on, too.'

'That sounds like fun.' He looked slightly wistful.

She was about to ask him if he was allowed to do that sort of thing, then remembered what he'd said about going to concerts and decided not to remind him about the restrictions in his life. Instead, she said, 'So are you a lark or an owl?'

'Owl,' he said. 'I'm all about sitting watching the stars.'

'In London?'

'You'd be surprised. There are a few sites in London where you can see the Milky Way at night,' he said. 'Maybe we can do that together some time.'

'I'd like that. I've always wanted to see the Northern Lights. Simon and I went to Iceland, but it rained for the whole week we were there and we weren't lucky enough to see them.'

'That's on my bucket list, too,' he said. 'Along with seeing Old Faithful in Yellowstone.'

'Good choice,' she said. 'We saw the Strokkur geyser in Iceland, and it was amazing, despite the rain.'

He smiled. 'So are you a lark or an owl?'

'Lark,' she said. 'I'm all about the sunrise. With the hours I work, it wouldn't be fair to have a dog—but if I did I'd take him for walks half an hour before sunrise, when the world is quiet and full of birdsong.'

By the time they'd finished their meal, Kelly felt she knew Luc a lot better. And, in other circumstances, she would have been tempted to forget all this fake stuff and date him properly. She *liked* the man she was getting to know; and he was definitely attractive, with those huge dark eyes and that killer smile. It shocked her, because she hadn't expected to have any feelings like this again. She'd been so caught up in work that she'd forgotten to have fun.

So maybe Luc was the one who could help her move on with her life.

But she knew that for him this was just a means to an end—persuading his parents to let him live the life he chose and continue making a difference to his patients. It wasn't a prelude to really dating each other. Today was simply letting them get to know each other so their stories would be straight if anyone asked awkward questions.

Luc pretty much underlined it when he said softly, 'Tell me about Simon.'

'We met at a party—a friend of a friend. He was an architect. He saw me home and we ended up spending the whole night talking. We started dating, but we pretty much knew each other was The One right from the beginning. We moved in together after six months and got married six months after that. He loved his job and he was really good at it.' She smiled. 'He used to run in the park every weekend and he cycled everywhere.'

'Did you join him?'

'No to the cycling, and I prefer to walk rather than run. But I was always happy to do long walks through London with him, looking at the buildings. And some of them are amazing—all you have to do is look up and you see things you never even knew existed.' She gave him a wry smile. 'We'd planned to extend our house and start a family. He'd drawn up all the plans, and the planning permission came through on the day he died.'

Luc reached across the table and squeezed her hand. 'I'm sorry.'

'It is as it is,' she said. 'I don't have any regrets about our life together. We were happy. I just wish we'd had more time—or that I'd had some idea about his heart condition so he'd had treatment for it. The only things I regret are the things we didn't get the chance to do.'

'I'm glad you were happy,' he said.

'Now I just want Jake and Summer to get the treatment they need. Jake followed Simon in a lot of things—he's an architect, too. But he and Millie started their family earlier than we planned to.'

'I'm still waiting to hear from their doctor,' Luc said. 'But I'll push again tomorrow.'

'Thank you.'

When they'd finished their coffee, Luc suggested walking through the water gardens.

'It's so pretty here,' Kelly said. 'As it's an Italian garden, does it remind you of home?'

'A bit—and I have to admit my own garden is an Italian one, with a fountain and topiary to give layers and height,' he said. He caught her fingers in his, startling her. 'If this is going to be a whirlwind romance,' he said as her eyes widened, 'people will expect me to hold your hand at the very least, and if you flinch every time we touch then everyone will know we're faking it.'

'Good point.' But this was the first time she'd held hands with a man since Simon, and it felt strange.

Clearly her feelings showed on her face, because he let her hand go and asked, 'Would you rather we stop this whole thing right now?'

She shook her head. 'I said I'd think about it. It's just…'

'I'm not Simon,' he said. 'And I'm taking this too fast for you.'

She winced. 'I'm sorry. I'm making a mess of this.'

'You're absolutely not,' he said. 'Let's keep walking.'

Kelly could understand why his girlfriends from a different background would find it hard to deal with the intrusiveness and all the protocols; but she didn't understand why someone from Luc's world couldn't relate to the other side of him, the doctor who needed to make a difference to the world for his best friend's sake. Her heart ached for him.

Would it be so hard for her to agree to help him? Just for a few short months? Or, if she agreed to help him with the clinic as well, would it get too complicated?

To distract herself, she said, 'I'm fitting an ICD to a six-year-old girl with Long QT Syndrome on Thursday. Are you around if there are complications?'

'I'm teaching,' he said, 'but if you need me I can be there.'

'I'll ask my patient's grandmother if your students can observe.'

'Thanks.' He looked at her. 'Given that you mentioned her grandmother, I presume there's a familial link?'

She nodded. 'Her mum. Who died.'

'That must be hard for you.'

'Dealing with a genetic cardiac condition that can be fatal? No, actually, it gives me hope that I can help people,' she said. 'Just... OK, I admit I get too involved. I want to save everyone, even though I know I can't.'

He took her hand and squeezed it. 'I know how that feels. But we do our best and that has to be enough.'

When Gino pulled up outside her flat, Kelly said to Luc, 'You and Gino are very welcome to come in for coffee.'

'Thanks, but I need to get back. See you tomorrow at work,' he said. 'And I'll see you at my place tomorrow night for dinner. Anything except red meat, right?'

'Right,' she said with a smile. 'Thanks for a lovely evening.'

'You're welcome. I've enjoyed getting to know you better.'

So had she. And that was worrying.

Luc spent the entire Wednesday working on a tricky coronary artery bypass graft, and didn't get a chance to see Kelly once he'd left the operating theatre. He texted her swiftly. I'll send Gino to pick you up.

It's fine. I'll get the Tube, she replied. Text me the address.

He did so, admiring her independent streak. And he'd really enjoyed her company last night. In other circumstances, he would've been tempted to ask her out properly. But he knew she wasn't ready to move on; the way she'd been so startled by him holding her hand was proof of that, and he could've kicked himself for being so insensitive. She hadn't agreed to marry him yet, and although they'd talked about making it look like a whirlwind courtship he'd taken things too fast. He needed to be patient. Even though he knew the clock was ticking for him.

And today would show her more of the other side of his life. Would it make her back away, the way Rachel had?

* * *

Luc was a prince. Of *course* he'd live in a mansion on the edge of Hampstead Heath, Kelly thought as she reached his address. And of course it would be a gated community where she'd have to check in with the concierge before she could even walk down his road.

The house was amazing—a new build, and yet with a nod to past architectural styles at the same time. Simon would've loved the Georgian symmetry of the three-storey facade, the shape of the roof, the dormer windows and the curved roof above the portico by the front door. There was a sweeping carriage drive in front of the house, and the garden was planted immaculately. Kelly felt a little like Cinderella; she definitely wasn't dressed up enough for this place.

But when Gino answered the front door to her, he was dressed in jeans.

And so was Luc, when she walked inside.

'Thank you for coming,' Luc said. 'Can I get you a drink?'

'A glass of water would be lovely.' And please don't let him put it into some fragile, priceless crystal that she'd end up dropping, she begged silently. 'And these are for you.' She handed him a bag. 'I forgot to ask if you'd prefer red or white, so I played it safe.'

'I love Sauvignon Blanc,' he said with a smile when he looked at the contents. 'And these are seriously good chocolates. Thank you very much.'

'It didn't feel quite right, bringing you flowers. Given your front garden, I think I made the right choice.'

'Maria—my housekeeper—had a hand in the planting. I admit, I don't really notice the flowers in the house, but she likes them. If my team's happy, then I'm happy.' He smiled at her. 'Would you like a guided tour before dinner?'

'Yes, please. I'd love to see this Italian garden you told me about yesterday.'

The interior of the house was even grander than the outside. The large living room had French doors, enormous sofas, a huge cream rug on the maple floors, and small occasional tables that held lamps and the largest vase of lilies she'd ever seen. And to think that if she agreed to his marriage of convenience she would be living here for a few months. She'd be terrified of breakages and spills whenever Susie and the twins came to visit.

Though she loved the large oil painting of a seascape on the living room wall. 'That's beautiful.'

'It's the view over the harbour from the castle in the Old Town in Bordimiglia,' he said.

The dining room was equally large, with a table big enough to seat twelve, and again it overlooked the garden. In the centre of the table was a huge vase of red tulips. 'They're gorgeous,' she said.

'Maria's favourites,' he said with a smile. 'And my mother's.'

'Mine, too.'

The kitchen was bigger than her entire flat, and everything was glossy white and gleaming chrome. The sort that would show every single fingerprint, she thought; this was definitely a high-maintenance house. There was a smaller table at one end of the kitchen, set for two.

'I thought we'd eat in here tonight—it's a bit cosier than the dining room,' Luc said. 'I tend to eat in here if it's just me.'

'Something smells very nice,' she said.

'My speciality,' he said.

There were a couple more sitting rooms, then a study lined with books and with a state-of-the-art computer on an otherwise clear desk, a comfy chair that was clearly his reading spot, and a small coffee table next to it stacked with medical journals. Next to that was a music room containing a baby grand piano, a couple of electric guitars on stands, and an amplifier.

'I'm expecting a demo,' she said.

'After dinner,' he promised. 'Though remember I warned you I'm not professional standard, and that wasn't false modesty.'

The hallway was massive, with marble flooring and a beautiful curving wrought-iron staircase. 'Bedrooms,' he said, 'all with en-suite bathrooms. The staff quarters are through here, on three floors.' He gestured to a corridor. 'The gym and pool are that way.' He led her down a different corridor. 'This is the garden room, for days when it's too wet to be outside.' The room was even bigger than the kitchen, with marble floors and comfortable chairs and what looked like orange trees in huge terracotta pots.

And from there he led her out into the garden. There was a huge stone terrace with a table and chairs, and massive pots containing bay trees and box hedges clipped into massive globes. Next to it was an English country garden full of colourful shrubs and late spring bulbs; beyond that lay a formal Italian garden complete with more neatly clipped topiary, marble statues and a fountain with stone dolphins.

'That's stunning,' she said.

He looked pleased. 'I love it out here.'

'And the Heath's just over there?'

'Behind the cypress trees,' he said.

'It's lovely, Luc.' And surprisingly homely, given the sheer scale of the place. She should've felt intimidated; she couldn't even begin to imagine how much the mortgage would be on a property like this. And yet the place was welcoming and full of warmth.

'I'm not going to rush you, but have a think about whether you could live here for a few months,' he said.

'I will,' she promised.

'Good. Come and have dinner,' he said, catching her fingers between his.

His speciality turned out to be macaroni cheese and greens, which he served with a heritage tomato salad and ciabatta bread.

'I'm impressed,' she said after her first taste. It was creamy without being sickly, and the cheese had a nice sharp bite to it. 'Tell me you made the bread as well.'

He wrinkled his nose. 'I'm not going to lie. That was Maria. But I did make the macaroni. Admittedly using dried pasta, but the sauce isn't from a jar.'

She smiled. 'Simon was a terrible cook. I always used to tease him that he could burn water. He could design the most gorgeous buildings, and if he did a quick scribbled sketch it looked like a flawless piece of art. But he always got too distracted to follow a recipe. The deal was that I cooked and he washed up.'

'Sounds fair, as long as you like cooking.'

'I do—it relaxes me,' she said.

'I have to admit I cheated and bought chocolate ganache pots for pudding,' he said.

'Considering how many hours you spent in Theatre today, you could've ordered in a takeaway or bought a meal from the supermarket and that would've been fine,' she said.

'No. I promised you I'd cook for you, and I keep my word,' he said.

'It's appreciated,' she said.

After dinner, they headed for the music room.

'So do you play the piano or anything?' he asked.

'No. Susie, Mum and I will sing our heads off to the radio or if we're watching a musical together. But none of us ever tried playing a musical instrument—well, except the recorder and the triangle at infant school, but that doesn't count.'

Luc sat down at the piano and patted the wide bench next to him. 'Give it a go. Let's try something.'

When she sat down, he lifted the lid and played four notes. 'Can you do that? Start at middle C,' he said, and pointed to the key in front of the keyhole.

Dubiously, she did so. Then she looked at him. 'I recognise that.'

'You said you were a Tom Hanks fan, so I hope you would.' He grinned. 'You're going to play that half and I'll do the melody. You repeat it four times—down two keys, down two keys, up one key, then back to the beginning.'

She did a couple of practice runs, getting it horribly wrong, but he got her to persevere. And then, when she was more confident, he joined in with the melody of 'Heart and Soul'.

'See? You can play,' he said.

'Barely. Play me something,' she urged.

He played a Mozart sonata she recognised, and some Bach. Then he looked at her. 'Eighties pop and nineties indie. I'll play, but you have to sing. Deal?'

'Deal.'

To her surprise, he played 'Come on Eileen'. She laughed. 'That always gets Mum up on

the dance floor.' She sang along with him, realising just how good his voice was.

'Your turn to choose,' he said.

'Eighties pop. So it's got to be Rick Astley
or Wham!' she said with a grin.

'As you wish.'

She looked at him, wondering if he was
teasing her with a reference to one of her favourite movies, but his face was deadpan.
Maybe that was because he was a prince and
had been taught to mask everything. She
wasn't going to overthink it.

He played 'Never Gonna Give You Up', followed by 'Wake Me Up Before You Go-Go'.
Between them, they sang nearly a dozen hits
from the eighties and nineties, with Luc ham-
ming it up and making Kelly laugh until her
stomach ached.

He finished with Oasis's 'Wonderwall', and
she let him sing it solo. When he played the
last note, he turned to her. His eyes were dark
and looked huge. And then he leaned forward
and brushed his mouth lightly against hers.
Not demanding, just gentle and so sweet that
it made her heart feel as if someone had just
squeezed it. At the same time, her mouth was
tingling where his lips had touched her skin.

He'd said he would give her time and not

rush her into a decision. And she knew he meant it, because he looked as shocked as she felt. Clearly this had been an impulse.

She could back away. Or she could kiss him back. And right at that moment she really wanted to kiss him. Would it be so bad if she gave in to the urge? She rested her palm against his cheek. 'Luc,' she said, and her voice sounded strangely rusty to her own ears.

He twisted his head so he could drop a kiss into her palm, and her stomach swooped.

It was the first time she'd wanted to kiss a man since Simon's death. The first time she'd wanted a man to kiss her. And this was a man who'd asked her to marry him in name only.

This shouldn't be happening.

As if her doubts showed on her face, he said softly, 'It's getting late. I'll drive you home.'

'Are you allowed?'

'Gino will drive, then. But I'll see you home.'

'Thank you.' She let her hand drop back into her lap. 'And for this evening. It's been fun.'

'I can't remember when I last enjoyed myself so much,' he said. 'You're good company, Kelly.'

'Even though I'm terrible at playing the piano?'

'Your singing makes up for it,' he said with

a smile. 'So. Tomorrow's whirlwind date. How about the cinema? You pick the film, and I'll arrange tickets.'

'Even if it's a soppy rom-com instead of an action movie?' she tested.

'OK. Theatre, then. Let's do a musical.'

'You're on. I'll organise tickets.'

'Actually, Gino will need to organise tickets.' He grimaced slightly.

Of course. His security detail would need to vet everything. 'OK. I don't mind what we see. Any music is a treat. But I'll pay for the tickets,' she said.

'I'll pay for the tickets,' he corrected. 'But you can buy me dinner, if it makes you feel better.'

'It does.'

This time, when Gino drove them home, Luc held Kelly's hand all the way. Again, he waited until she was indoors before they drove off. And Kelly felt as if the dried-up edges of her life were starting to soften again. Sitting at the piano with him that evening, singing and laughing together... She'd felt happier than she had in a long, long time.

And for a second she could almost feel Simon's arms round her, giving her a hug. Hear him whisper, 'Be happy.'

She shook herself. How fanciful. She didn't believe in ghosts.

Besides, Luc wasn't the one to make her love again. This was a temporary favour to buy time for both of them, and she really mustn't get carried away and forget it.

CHAPTER SIX

ON THURSDAY NIGHT, Luc took Kelly for dinner at a small Italian restaurant after work.

'As you didn't call me, I'm assuming your ICD went well?' he asked.

'Very. How was your teaching day?' she asked.

'Good. Oh, and I have some news for you. Obviously I can't discuss confidential medical information, but you might want to check in with Jake and Summer and ask them if they have some news for you.'

Her eyes widened. 'Are you telling me they're on the trial?'

'As I said, I can't discuss confidential medical information,' he repeated. 'But Jake isn't under the same constraints as I am. He can tell you all the details that I can't.'

'Thank you. You have no idea how much this means.'

'The judgement was made purely on a clinical basis,' he said. 'As a surgeon, I have to be impartial and keep emotions out of it.'

'I know. But you could've refused even to consider them. And I feel a lot better knowing that they're both going to get more check-ups than usual.'

'With proper treatment and follow-up, most patients with HCM live a normal life,' he reminded her gently. 'I'm sorry that Simon was unlucky.'

'Yes.' She blew out a breath. 'I'm not going mopey on you.'

'I know, but that news was bound to make you feel emotional. I probably should've handled it better,' he admitted.

'You're a good man, Luc,' she said, and reached across the table to squeeze his hand.

He was going to have to be careful. Their relationship was a total fake. He really couldn't allow himself to react to her touch like this. Growing up as a prince, he'd learned to keep his feelings private and wear a public mask of smiles. Whatever was happening in your private life, you just got on with your duty. This was the same thing. If Kelly agreed to it—and he really hoped she would—there would be a time limit. After that, they'd have a quiet divorce and they'd be strictly friends and colleagues. Letting himself fall in love with her wasn't part of the deal.

'Les Mis!' she said as they reached the theatre. 'This is always a treat.' She beamed at him. 'Thank you so much, Luc. Though I hope you brought tissues. I always cry. Especially at "On My Own" and "I Dreamed a Dream".'

'You've seen it more than once, then?'

'Susie and Ange love musicals as much as I do. So does Mum, so I've seen it with all three of them—separately and together. And I organised a team night out to see it, about five years ago.'

He winced. 'Sorry. I should've guessed that you'd already seen it, or at least checked with you first.'

'I would've still said yes, because I absolutely love this show,' she said, and reached up to kiss his cheek.

How easy it would be to turn and face her properly, and to change that kiss on the cheek into something more sensual.

Luc kept himself firmly in check, and ushered her into the theatre.

'We've got a box?' she asked, looking surprised when he led her up the stairs.

He shrugged. 'It keeps Gino happy.'

'Got it.' She squeezed his hand. 'We have amazing legroom and a fantastic view—we're looking down so we can see the patterns of the choreography as well.'

Typical Kelly, looking on the bright side instead of being disappointed that she wasn't among the crowd like everyone else. He appreciated that.

As she'd predicted, Kelly cried during the sad songs, and he had to borrow a handkerchief from Gino to help her mop them up. And this time, after Gino had driven them back to her place, Luc accepted her offer to come in for coffee. Gino, too, accepted, but insisted on sitting at the kitchen table rather than with them in the living room.

'It feels rude, leaving you out here on your own, Gino. You're my guest,' Kelly said.

'I'm working,' Gino said gently. 'But thank you for looking after me so well.' He gestured to the tin she'd brought out of the cupboard. 'I love cannoli wafers. And your coffee's good.' He patted her arm. 'Go and chat to Luc, *bella*. You both know where I am if you need me.'

Luc followed Kelly into the living room. The walls were painted a bright sunny yellow; there was a bookcase stuffed with a mix of medical textbooks and novels, a comfortable sofa with a coffee table next to it and a small television. There were a lot of framed photographs on the mantelpiece. 'May I?' he asked, gesturing to them.

'Of course.' She came to stand beside him and talked him through them. 'That's my sister Susie, on her wedding day to Nick, both of them with the twins just before last Christmas because they always do a family portrait, Mum and Dad with me on my graduation day, and Simon and me on our wedding day.'

They looked so happy together. Luc's heart ached for her. He'd felt bad enough when Rachel had broken off their relationship but they hadn't even got to the engagement stage. How much worse it must have been for Kelly to marry the love of her life and then lose him before they could start their longed-for family—and it was an extra twist of the knife that Simon had died from an undiagnosed cardiac condition, when Kelly was a cardiologist.

It was clear to him that she hadn't moved on from loving Simon. That she might never be ready to move on. Which meant he felt a lot less guilty about asking her to help him; she wasn't going to be taking a risk with her heart because it still belonged to Simon. No way was she going to fall for him and get hurt.

'They're lovely photos,' he said. 'Who's this with you?'

'Angela—my best friend. We met on the first

day of sixth form. That's us at our prom.' She smiled. 'We look so young there.'

'And beautiful.'

'I wasn't fishing,' she said.

'I know.' The words had slipped out before he could stop them. He really needed to get a grip. 'What would you like to do tomorrow?'

'I'm working, and I think you might be co-opted onto the team pub quiz,' she said. 'But I was thinking—on Saturday, my parents are having a barbecue.' She looked at him. 'And I was wondering if you'd like to meet my family.'

He went very still. Did that mean she was going to agree to help him? Or was this kind of the last test—if her family liked him, then she'd agree to the marriage of convenience?

'I'd like that,' he said carefully.

'Good.' She smiled. 'My family's nice, Luc. They'll ask you a gazillion questions, but it'll be relatively easy to deflect them if we keep the story as close to the truth as possible. We met just over a month ago when Sanjay asked me to show you round on your first day, and we liked each other. We've been on a couple of dates.'

He sucked in a breath. 'So, the whirlwind courtship?'

'Yes. I'll help you,' she said.

'Thank you. I know it's a big ask.'

'I still have my doubts,' she admitted. 'But you're helping me. I'm not *quite* as much of a workaholic as I was even a month ago, and the new procedures you've brought into the department have reinvigorated my love of medicine—I'm doing my job because I love it, not because I'm scared of losing someone. So I want to help you, too. And that includes your new clinic. It's the fresh start I think I need.'

'That's fantastic news. Thank you. I really appreciate it.' He paused. 'So what can I bring to the barbecue?'

'Just yourself.'

He shook his head. 'That's not how I was brought up. Wine, flowers, chocolates?'

'Dad's just been diagnosed as diabetic, so not chocolate,' she said. 'Flowers and wine would be very nice. Not too—' She grimaced and cut off the words. 'Sorry. That was about to sound really ungrateful and I don't mean it that way.'

'Not too showy-offy,' he guessed. 'Noted. And you weren't ungrateful.'

'Just… My family's very ordinary.'

'Actually,' he said, 'behind the image, so's mine. You'd get on well with my sisters. My parents would like you, too.'

Once he'd finished his coffee, he turned to her. 'I'd better get going.'

'Thank you again for this evening, Luc. I really enjoyed it.'

'Me, too,' he said. He leaned forward and kissed her very lightly on the lips. 'Good night.'

'Good night.'

Her pupils looked huge, and he wondered whether she was feeling that same unexpected spark as he was. But he wasn't going to make things difficult by asking.

He was still thinking about it when Gino drove him home.

'All right, boss?' Gino asked. He'd been with Luc for ten years, long enough to know him well and comfortable enough in his position to ask awkward questions.

'Yes,' Luc fibbed.

'I like her,' Gino said.

'She's a good colleague. A friend,' Luc said.

'You don't look at each other as if you're just friends,' Gino pointed out.

That was a good thing. It meant they'd be able to convince her family at the weekend and he'd uphold his half of the deal. But on the other hand it was a bad thing. It wasn't supposed to be more than friendship, and he couldn't afford to let things get out of hand.

The last thing he wanted was for Kelly to get hurt. 'Maybe,' Luc said casually.

Thankfully Gino didn't push it any further. And everything between himself and Kelly felt totally as usual at work the next day.

On Saturday, it was raining.

Luc rang Kelly. 'Given the weather, do I assume the barbecue is cancelled?'

'Absolutely not. Dad's been known to sit in pouring rain, holding a massive golf umbrella over himself and the barbecue—on more than one occasion. If it was snowing in the middle of June, he'd still insist on having a barbecue.' She laughed. 'The twins will be there. I hope you don't mind children.'

'I like children just fine,' he said. 'I'm an uncle to two, remember. Which means I have an amazing line of bad jokes.'

'That's good. I'll see you in a couple of hours, then.'

This was ridiculous, being nervous, Kelly told herself sharply. Luc wasn't the first man she'd taken home to meet her family.

But he was the first man she'd taken home since Simon's death.

And she needed to make this convincing, because she was about to tell her family an enormous white lie. Not to hurt them, but to give her a breathing space from the nagging and to stop them worrying about her.

She was still jittery by the time Luc rang her doorbell.

He frowned. 'What's wrong?'

'I feel guilty,' she said. 'About what we're doing.'

'You're not doing anything wrong. You're doing me a massive favour,' he reminded her.

'I know.' She bit her lip.

'You're taking me to meet your family, so they can see for themselves that I'm not going to make you unhappy.' He smiled at her. 'If we turn up with you looking anxious, that's pretty much going to wreck our cover story.'

'I guess.'

'I could tell you terrible jokes all the way to your parents' house.'

'I think I'll manage,' she said.

'Good. Let's go.'

'Let me get everything out of the fridge.' She'd made salads earlier and put them into storage boxes.

Luc helped her into the car. 'I brought half a case of wine and some flowers for your parents. I hope that's acceptable.'

She looked at the bouquet of peonies and pink gypsophilia. 'Mum will *love* those.'

'Not too showy-offy?' he checked.

She winced. 'Sorry. It's hard for you. I imagine people expect the Prince to turn up with things gift-wrapped in pure gold. But it's the cardiac surgeon my family's meeting.'

'It's a strange line to walk,' he agreed. 'Thank you, Kelly. For making me feel real.'

Right at that moment, the uncertainty in his eyes made her want to lean forward and kiss him, reassure him that everything was going to be just fine.

And, even though she felt nervous about it, she didn't want him to feel bad. So she leaned forward and brushed her mouth against his. 'You'll do.'

Her mouth tingled, flustering her slightly; but she could see the same thing in his expression.

This was strange. A fake relationship that needed to look real—yet, at the same time, was starting to feel real.

Could this really be the start of something they both weren't expecting?

She pushed the thoughts aside. It wasn't going to work out that way.

As she'd half expected, her family was gathered in the large farmhouse kitchen that also doubled as the dining room.

'Mum, Dad, I'd like you to meet Luc Bianchi. Luc, my parents, Caroline and Robin, my sister Susie and her husband Nick, and the twins, Oscar and Jacob,' she introduced them swiftly.

'Delighted to meet you all,' he said, and handed Caroline the bouquet and the box of wine to Robin.

'How gorgeous! Thank you,' Caroline said, and gave him a hug. 'Nice to meet you, Luc.'

'Yes, good to meet you. And thank you for the wine.' Robin shook his hand.

'Wait a second—aren't you…?' Susie asked, looking shocked.

'Yes,' Luc said. 'Prince Luciano of Bordimiglia. Otherwise known as Luc Bianchi, cardiac surgeon.'

'So do we call you "Your Highness"?' Nick asked as he shook hands with Luc.

He smiled. 'No. Luc's fine. Um, I do have my driver with me outside, if I could perhaps have a parking permit for the car?'

'You're very welcome to a parking permit,' Caroline said, 'but your driver is most certainly not waiting outside. There's plenty of room here and plenty of food, so I'd be happier if he joined us.' She winced. 'Oh—is that allowed?'

'It is. And thank you,' Luc said.

'Come with me, and we'll sort out the parking,' Robin said. 'Actually, then I'm going to put you to work doing barbecue stuff with me and Nick.'

Luc grinned. 'I've already heard the story about the barbecues in the rain under the golf umbrella.'

'They always make me come inside if it starts thundering,' Robin said, looking disgusted. 'We're all going to take turns doing the manly jobs. Barbecuing, umbrella-holding and twin-wrangling.'

'Count me in. Oscar and Jacob, I have a question for you,' Luc said. 'Why did the cake visit the doctor?'

'I don't know,' the twins chorused shyly.

'Because it was feeling crummy,' Luc said.

Kelly winked at Luc to show her approval: it was about the best thing he could have done. The boys and her father all loved corny jokes.

Robin clapped him on the back. 'I must remember that for the office on Monday. I think you and I are going to get on famously, Luc.'

'You,' Susie said to Kelly as soon as Luc was out of earshot, 'have some explaining to do.'

'Luc's a cardiothoracic surgeon,' Kelly said. 'He started at the hospital about five weeks ago. Sanjay asked me to show him round the department and take him to lunch, the first day, because he was in meetings.' So far, all so true.

'And you're dating him?' Caroline said. 'But...'

'But nothing. The pair of you are constantly throwing eligible men at me. Shouldn't you be pleased that I'm dating someone?'

'He's a *prince*,' Susie said.

'A very low-key one who sees himself as a surgeon first,' Kelly pointed out.

'But what about when he has to take over from his father?' Caroline asked.

'He doesn't want to be King. He's trying to persuade his father to change the succession laws so his oldest sister can take over. And I have to say he's a brilliant surgeon. I've sat in on a couple of his ops. And,' Kelly added, 'he's doing a trial of new treatment for HCM. Jake called me the other day to tell me that he and Summer are going to be on it.'

'Oh, darling. That's great news.' Caroline hugged her. 'I take it Luc knows about Simon?'

'Yes. Actually, HCM is why he became a doctor. His best friend died from it when they were fifteen. So he understands why I wanted Jake and Summer on the trial—though that's strictly because they met the trial guidelines and not because I asked him.'

Susie hugged her, too. 'OK. But even though he's a doctor, Kel, he's still a prince.'

'A doctor first,' Kelly said. 'He plans to go back to Bordimiglia in two years' time and set up a state-of-the-art cardiac clinic.'

'So where does that leave you, if he's not staying here?' Susie asked.

'It's early days,' Kelly said. 'Though he's going to need a good cardiologist.'

Caroline looked shocked. 'You mean you'd go with him?'

'It's a good opportunity, and maybe that's what I need to help me move on,' Kelly said. 'A change of scene. No memories.'

'It's a long way away,' Caroline said.

'I know. But nothing's set in stone,' Kelly said.

'Obviously the paparazzi haven't got wind of you dating him, yet,' Susie said.

'No, but it'll be fine,' Kelly reassured her.

'But he's a *prince*, Kel.' Susie looked worried.

'A surgeon,' Kelly said firmly. 'Give him a chance. You might like him. Mum, where do you want me to put these salads?'

Luc was touched by how easily Kelly's family made him feel at home. They were clearly treating him as a surgeon rather than a prince, and he appreciated that. He was kept busy alternately manning the barbecue, holding the golf umbrella over whoever was manning the barbecue next, ferrying cooked food indoors and keeping the twins out of mischief, working as a team with Robin and Nick.

And how good it felt to be treated as a normal person, as part of a normal family. Though, at the same time, it made him feel guilty. He'd pretty much pushed his own family away in an attempt to be his own person; although he was close to his sisters, his relationship with his parents was much trickier, and he knew they all hid behind the excuse of his parents' royal schedule. He needed to make more of an effort to find a compromise. The kind of relationship Kelly had with her family was exactly what he wanted. Just he didn't quite know how to make that work.

The rain stopped, and while he was manning the barbecue Kelly came over with a plate of salad and a glass of wine.

'I've been despatched to make sure the cook's OK,' she said with a smile.

'Very OK.' On impulse, he stole a kiss. 'Thank you for inviting me.'

She went slightly pink. 'Pleasure.'

'Your family's lovely,' he said softly. 'I appreciate the fact they're seeing me for myself and not my position.'

'Expect to be grilled later,' she warned. 'But they like you.'

'Good.' He stole another kiss. Because that was what a new boyfriend would do, wasn't it? The fact that he actually wanted to kiss Kelly was completely beside the point.

And it was good to eat a normal family meal in a normal family environment. When Oscar fell over and scraped his knee, Luc was the nearest and scooped him up to deal with it and talked to him about knights in armour to distract him from the sting of the antiseptic.

And, just as Kelly had warned, Susie insisted that they should do the washing up together after the meal while everyone sat out in the garden, now the rain had lifted. Grilling time, he thought. 'You're Kelly's big sister. Mine would be the same and want to be sure whoever I brought home had good intentions,' he said. 'So what do you want to know?'

'You're dating my little sister,' Susie said.

'I am,' he agreed. It wasn't the whole truth, but enough to count.

'And you know about her past.'

'I know how much she loved Simon and how devastated she was at losing him. So I understand why you're all worried about her. I'll be careful with her,' he said. He smiled. 'Just to reassure you, I think a lot of your sister. I respect her professionally and personally.'

Susie looked wary. 'But your world is very different from ours, Luc.'

'I'm a heart surgeon,' he said softly. 'So, actually, my world is pretty much the same as Kelly's. We work in the same department. Sometimes she sits in when I operate on her patients, and sometimes I ask her to run tests on mine.'

'Except she's an ordinary woman and you also happen to be a prince. Can I be honest?' At his nod, she said, 'The newspapers can be unkind. That worries me.'

'The media can be vile,' he agreed, 'but there's nothing about your family they can use to hurt her.'

'You checked us out?'

This was where he needed to reassure her properly. 'Yes—for Kelly's sake. As you say, the newspapers can be unkind. I've been there before and it ended badly,' he said softly. 'I mean to take care of Kelly and make sure the press can't hurt her—or, by extension, any of your family and close friends. I admit, there probably will be some press intrusion, and I apologise in advance for that. But our press team will be there to support you. Anything you need, you'll have it. I'll make sure you, Nick and your parents have all the relevant phone numbers before I leave today. They'll be available to you twenty-four-seven.'

Susie still looked worried. 'Gino's a nice man, but he's your bodyguard.'

'Which I know is a strange thing if you didn't grow up with it, but I'm used to it. He's part of my team. And my team's protection will extend to Kelly,' he said.

'You're the first man she's actually brought home since Simon, so it's obvious that you matter to her,' Susie said.

Guilt lanced through him. Kelly's family was nice, and they really loved her. They were close. Whereas his own family was nice, and he'd distanced himself from them. It made him feel selfish and horrible. 'She wanted me to meet you.'

'Because you matter,' Susie repeated.

'Because she loves you all, and she doesn't want you to worry about her.' That much was true. He wanted to stick to the truth as much as he could. 'And of course you'll worry,' he added gently. 'But I promise you I won't hurt her.'

'OK.' Susie took a deep breath. 'And this clinic you want to set up?'

So Kelly had mentioned it to her family,

then. 'My best friend died from HCM when
we were fifteen. It's why I became a cardiac specialist—I saw what his family went
through and I wanted to save other people
from that, I guess, and to save other fifteen-
year-olds losing their best friends, the way I
did,' he added wryly. 'I want to set up a cutting-edge cardiac clinic in Bordimiglia.' He
paused. What he needed to give Kelly's family
was some reassurance that he wasn't going to
whisk her off with him right this very second.
'I asked Kelly if she would consider coming
back with me and training the next generation of cardiologists. But it's still a couple of
years away—I wouldn't leave Muswell Hill
Memorial Hospital in the lurch by accepting
this post and then disappearing in a couple of
weeks to set up my new clinic. I plan to spend
a couple of years in my current role, getting
more experience, and give them plenty of time
to replace me.'

'That's fair,' she said. 'But Bordimiglia's a
long way from England.'

'A couple of hours on a plane,' he said.
'Which is just as quick as if, say, she'd moved
to Manchester and you took the train to see
her.'

Susie nodded. 'And I guess she has a point.
Working in a place where there are no memo-

ries might help her move on. And that's all we want—for her to be happy again.'

'I understand,' he said softly.

'I apologise for the grilling.'

'No apology needed. It's good that her family looks out for her. My sisters will probably grill her in the same way at some point.' He smiled. 'But actually as soon as they meet her they'll see her for who she is and they'll love her.'

When Susie and Luc reappeared from the kitchen, to Kelly's relief they both looked relaxed rather than awkward. And Luc was fine about the idea of taking the twins to the park to play football. It made her heart squeeze sharply—Simon had been a fantastic uncle and had loved going to the park with the boys—but she appreciated that Luc was making the effort to fit in with her family.

Susie hugged Kelly as they stood on the sidelines, watching the men play football with the twins. 'I really like him. He's a lot more down to earth than I would have expected from someone in his position. Nick and Dad like him, too.'

'And Mum?' Kelly checked.

'She's as worried as I am,' Susie admitted, 'but he pretty much reassured me—'

'—when you grilled him in the kitchen,' Kelly finished.

'A man who doesn't complain about helping with the washing up or being grilled by a bossy older sister is one to keep hold of,' Susie said. 'We all just want to see you happy.'

'I am,' Kelly promised.

In a weird way, this thing with Luc was helping her to move on. She'd never forget Simon and she'd always love him, but she was starting to think that she could move on and find happiness again.

On the Wednesday, Luc's patient Maia Isley was scheduled to have the new personalised external aortic root support treatment. Kelly had already been involved in the scans where they'd made a 3D computer model of Maia's heart, and Luc was happy with the tailored mesh support that he was going to wrap round her aorta. His colleague from his old department had come over to lend a hand with the operation, and Sanjay joined Kelly to watch the operation.

'So today we're making history,' Sanjay said.

'It's wonderful to be part of new developments,' Kelly agreed.

And it was wonderful to watch Luc operating. She noticed how deft his hands were and how his confidence and clear direction made the rest of the team relax. Maia had agreed to let them film the operation to use for training in the department, for their colleagues who couldn't be there to see it.

'It's amazing how far we've come since I was your age,' Sanjay said.

She grinned. 'You're not that old, Sanj.'

'Sometimes I feel it,' he said. 'I'm glad Luc's joined us. I did worry that we might have a problem with press intrusion, but his PR team has been excellent.'

She'd remember to tell that to her parents and Susie later, to help ease any worries they might have. And what she and Luc were planning might still have an effect on the hospital; but hopefully Luc's team could spin it positively.

'Are you OK?' Sanjay asked.

'Sure. Just a bit overwhelmed by what we're doing here today,' she said. Which was true… Just not the whole truth.

'You and Luc seem to be getting on really well,' Sanjay said.

'He's a good man. I like him a lot.'

'Agreed,' Sanjay said.

And if her boss had noticed that they were

getting on well... Then hopefully they'd manage to convince everyone at work that their marriage was real.

CHAPTER SEVEN

THE FOLLOWING WEEKEND, Kelly sorted out the
final arrangements for New York with Luc.

'Do you want me to pack hand luggage
only?' she asked.

'No. Bring whatever you like,' he said.

'Are you sure? Packing luggage for the hold
means we'll have to wait around for the plane
to unload.'

'Not quite,' he said.

She frowned. 'How come?'

'We're using a private jet,' he explained.

She felt her eyes widen. 'You own a plane?'

'No. I'm chartering a flight.' He shrugged,
as if it wasn't a big deal. 'It makes life a lot
easier for Gino and the team.'

Security. Of course. She should've thought
of that.

'So we're going to New York tomorrow—
just you and me?' she checked.

'And three of my security team. You haven't

met Federico and Vincenzo yet,' he said, 'but they're nice.'

'Right.'

'They've known me for years and they're as discreet as Gino. You'll hardly know they're there,' he reassured her.

But it brought home to her just how unusual his life was. How odd hers was going to be, once she'd married him. 'OK,' she said, the doubts flooding through her.

'Are you OK with flying?' he asked.

'I've never been in a private jet,' she said, 'but I'm assuming it's super-safe or Gino wouldn't let you set foot on it.'

He smiled. 'Exactly.'

The enormity of what they were about to do filled her head. 'You're not having second thoughts about all this?'

'No,' he said, sounding perfectly serene and confident. Then he looked at her. 'Are you?'

'Yes,' she admitted. She'd told her parents that Luc was taking her away for a few days, but had told a white lie in saying that she didn't know where.

'Your family have met me, and it went just fine,' he reminded her. 'I understand that they'll be upset at not being included in the wedding, but I'll take the blame for whisking you off your feet. If they want some kind of celebration when we get back, I can organise that,' he added. 'And I'll buy you a dress when we're out there.'

'Are you sure this isn't going to land you in a huge amount of trouble?' she asked.

'There will probably be a bit of a row,' he said, 'but nothing I can't handle. Sometimes you just have to step out of a box to help other people think outside of that same box.' He kissed her lightly. 'Don't worry. It's going to be fine. And I really appreciate what you're doing for me.'

On Monday morning, Kelly was packed and waiting when Luc rang her doorbell at six a.m.

'Ready?' he asked.

'Ready,' she fibbed, and locked the door to her old life behind her.

Luc insisted on carrying her case to the car. 'Gino you already know; this is Federico and Vincenzo,' he introduced her swiftly.

'Good morning,' she said shyly.

Travelling with Luc's entourage was nothing like anything she'd experienced before. At the airport, there was no queueing to drop off baggage, or for security and passport control, not even for boarding. Everything was smooth and efficient.

The plane itself was amazing: wide, comfortable seats with plenty of legroom, work tables, a large galley and washroom, and access to all their baggage.

Now she understood why he'd said that luggage wouldn't be a problem. And she could also understand how the ordinary women Luc had dated had felt overwhelmed by this side of his life, because she was feeling pretty much that way, too.

'OK?' he asked.

'Right now, I'm feeling a tiny bit out of my depth,' she admitted.

'I'm sorry. It's not meant to be that way.'

'I know.' She squeezed his hand. 'You're not trying to be showy-offy. This is just how your world is.'

'Thank you for understanding.' Though his dark eyes were filled with concern.

'It's all right, Luc. I know what I'm doing. Ish,' she said. 'I'm not going to let you down.' On impulse, she kissed his cheek, and his pupils were huge as he looked at her.

'If there's anything at all I can do to make this easier, just say.'

Short of flying her entire family over to be there for the wedding—and then it would be massively unfair to leave his family out, plus this was going to be a marriage in name only rather than a real one—there was nothing he could do. Though she appreciated the offer. 'It's fine,' she said.

'OK. Our flight lasts for eight hours and we leave at seven, so we'll arrive in New York at three p.m. our time—that's ten a.m. US time,' he told her.

'Got it,' she said.

The flight was the most comfortable Kelly had ever experienced. The captain came to introduce himself and his cabin staff, and then they served the most amazing breakfast: freshly squeezed orange juice, exotic fruit, smoked salmon and scrambled egg on rye bagels, and truly excellent coffee.

They all watched a movie, played several board games—and Kelly really liked the fact that Gino, Federico and Vincenzo all played competitively rather than letting Luc win—and then finally they landed in New York and were whisked through security.

She sent a text to her parents, Susie and Angela to tell them she'd arrived safely.

New York! How lovely. Have a wonderful time, darling, was her mum's response.

Amazing! Have fun in the Big Apple and fingers crossed you get to see a Broadway show, was Susie's.

But Angela's reply made Kelly bite her lip.

Are you sure about all this? Not too late to change your mind xx.

Oh, but it was. She'd promised to help Luc. Backing out now would be mean. And he was right—they weren't hurting anyone. She hadn't introduced him to Angela yet. Her friend clearly didn't approve of their plan and she didn't want to cause any unnecessary friction.

There was a limo waiting outside, which took them to a gorgeous white stone building on Fifth Avenue, twenty storeys stretching up into the blue sky.

She blinked. 'I recognise this building.'

He smiled at her. 'As a Tom Hanks fan, of course you would.'

'*Sleepless in Seattle*,' she said. 'Luc, this is—'

He pressed one finger to her lip. 'I know. And I can afford it, so don't worry. If we're going to elope, I thought we should do it in style.'

And how, she thought, in one of the poshest hotels in New York, right on Central Park. 'OK. And thank you.'

A bellboy in a black uniform and wearing a black brimless cap shaped like a drum took their luggage up to their room. Again, it was a million miles away from the small and ordinary hotel room Kelly would normally have booked. They actually had a suite, with two bedrooms, two bathrooms and a sitting room overlooking Central Park.

'Gino, Vincenzo and Federico also have rooms on our floor, and they'll need to check out our suite first whenever we come back to it,' Luc said. 'I'm sorry for the intrusiveness.'

'Don't apologise. It's necessary,' she said. 'But it must be hard for you, always having to be aware of security.'

'I grew up with it, so I don't know any different,' he said. 'Pick whichever room you'd like.'

'Are you sure?'

'Very sure,' he said with a smile.

'Thank you.'

The bedrooms were both gorgeous, but Kelly chose the one with the view of the park. There was a separate bathroom with a mosaic floor and walls; as well as a king-sized bed, the bedroom contained a sofa and a desk with a gilded Louis XIV chair. The decor was white and grey and navy, with accents of gold; though the overall effect was stylish rather than overpowering.

'This is amazing,' she said.

'I'm glad you like it. I'll give you time to freshen up,' he said, 'and then we can go and finalise the paperwork to get our wedding licence. Then we'll have the rest of the day to explore.'

'OK.' Kelly discovered that the shower in her bathroom had jets of water coming out of the wall, as well as a massive shower-head that worked as a spray or as a waterfall. How her mum, sister and best friend would love this.

Mindful of the time, she was quick to shower and change, and she was grateful when Gino handed her a takeaway cup of coffee in the limo. 'To keep you going, *bella*,' he said with a smile.

'*Grazie,*' she said, smiling back.

The limo took them to the Manhattan City Clerk's Office Marriage Bureau. Luc had already completed most of the paperwork online to save them some time. Their passports acted as their photo ID, and Kelly had brought along the original copies of her marriage certificate to Simon and his death certificate. Taking them out of the folder made her catch her breath.

Luc looked at Kelly, and it suddenly registered with him what she was holding. Her marriage certificate and Simon's death certificate.

Of course this was going to be hard for her.

Guilt flooded through him. So much for his good intentions. This was hurting her anyway.

He took her hand. 'Kelly. I'm sorry. I didn't mean for this to be hard for you.'

'It's all right.'

But her eyes were a little bit too bright.

'You don't have to do this,' he said. 'We can call it off right now.'

She gave him a wry smile. 'Considering how much planning's gone into this—not to mention that we've flown thousands of miles to get here, and how much money this has cost—it'd be a bit daft for me to back out now.'

'Money isn't important. You are.' It shocked him to realise how important she'd become to him, but he shoved the thought aside. Not now. 'We can call it off.'

'I said I'd help you.'

'But it's not meant to be at a personal cost to you.'

'It's fine. Just…' She swallowed hard. 'I guess this is one way to make myself move on.'

'Not if you're not ready,' he said firmly. 'I won't do that to you.'

And it was a lesson to him, too, not to get carried away. Not to want what she wasn't ready to give anyone. He'd really have to keep a lid on the pull of attraction he felt towards her. It would make everything much too complicated.

'I'm fine.' She nodded. 'Really. I made a promise and I'm going to keep it.' She gave him a small smile.

Finally, the licence was processed and Luc tucked it safely away in his wallet. 'Time for some shopping,' he said.

'Not all women love shopping, you know,' she pointed out. 'Though I do need to get some souvenirs for Mum, Dad, Susie, Nick, the twins, Ange and Rod.'

'I have your mum, Susie and Angela covered,' he said, 'and we can find things for everyone else when we do the touristy stuff.'

'What do you mean, Mum, Susie and Angela are covered?' she asked.

He wrinkled his nose. 'I can't tell you without spoiling a surprise for you. But trust me on this.'

Kelly realised that she *did* trust him. She knew the surgeon and it looked as if she was going to get to know the prince.

'We'll do just two shops today,' he said. 'We need wedding rings and your dress.'

How different it was going to be from her last wedding, when her mum and her sister and her best friend had gone dress-shopping with her and they'd made a day of it, including lunch and afternoon tea. Again, the memory put a lump in her throat. But this wasn't a real marriage, she reminded herself. She and Luc didn't love each other the way she and Simon had. They were friends, and they were just helping each other to solve a problem. None of this was real; the marriage would be in name only.

She wasn't that surprised when the limo took them to Fifth Avenue. On the corner was a store she'd seen in plenty of photographs, with the words 'Tiffany & Co.' carved into the door's lintel, and an iconic statue of Atlas holding a clock above that. Inside was a massive sales floor and a huge sweeping staircase.

'It's the first time I've ever been here,' she said. 'It's incredible. Just how I imagined it. No wonder Holly Golightly was so entranced by this place.'

He smiled and took her hand. 'Let's get what we need.'

With the help of the sales girl, they both chose very plain platinum wedding bands.

'You should have an engagement ring, too,' Luc said thoughtfully.

'There's no need. We're not actually getting engaged,' she reminded him.

'This is meant to be a whirlwind romance,

so you need an engagement ring.' He smiled. 'There's a cafe here now, so maybe we should've come here first and had breakfast at Tiffany's—apart from the fact that we've already had breakfast, and our day started in the middle of the night here.'

She smiled. 'That film always makes me sob buckets.'

'The bit with the cat. It's the same with my sisters,' he said.

Would she ever meet his family? Or would they cast him out for marrying someone well below his social status? Her doubts came flooding back again. 'What if your parents disown you?'

'They won't disown me. I love them and they love me—there's just this one sticking point, which we're sorting out.'

And if he'd misjudged this and they did disown him, she thought, then she'd ask for an audience—or whatever you did with royalty— and tell his parents that he was a good man and a brilliant surgeon, and he deserved better from them.

He chose a heart-shaped diamond on a plain platinum shank to go with her wedding band. 'Given our jobs,' he said softly, 'this is appropriate—and I want you to keep it afterwards.'

'But…' There hadn't been a price on it, so she hated to think how much it had cost.

'No buts. You're giving me the chance to do what I love, and this is the very least I can do,' he said firmly. 'Think of it as a token of my esteem.'

'Normal people don't buy their friends super-expensive jewellery. Even if they are a hot-shot heart surgeon.'

'You're getting both sides of me for the time being,' he reminded her. 'And now, I think, lunch.'

They ended up grabbing a snack in the cafe at Tiffany's, and then the whirlwind stuff started in earnest.

'Romantic touristy things are the order of the day,' Luc insisted, and the result was a horse and carriage ride through Central Park.

Kelly thoroughly enjoyed the carriage ride, and she didn't have to fake her smile when Luc took a selfie of them with his arm round her shoulders. Right at that moment, she couldn't think of anyone she would rather have shared it with. Then Luc asked the driver to stop by the entrance to one of the gardens. 'Let's go for a little stroll here,' he said, and helped Kelly out of the carriage. 'It's the Shakespeare garden, so all the plants are inspired by his plays. There used to be a white mulberry tree here, that was apparently from his garden.'

It was stunning, with trees covered in pink and white blossom and beds full of late spring flowers. Luc paused by a bed full of bright red tulips. 'I think,' he said, 'this is the place.' Then he took the duck-egg-blue box out of his pocket. 'Where better to get engaged than here?'

To Kelly's surprise, he actually dropped down on one knee.

'Dr Phillips, would you do me the honour of becoming my wife tomorrow?' he asked softly.

For a crazy moment, this whole wedding thing actually felt real. As if Luc was asking her to share his life properly, rather than in name only for the short time they agreed to.

'I...' Her mouth went dry. 'Yes.'

He smiled up at her, and it felt as if her heart had done an anatomically impossible backflip. Then he rose to his feet again and slipped the heart-shaped diamond onto her ring finger.

And then he kissed her.

Slow and sweet and heady, and her head was spinning slightly when he broke the kiss. She didn't think it was the jet lag, either: it was all Luc. Those sensual dark eyes, that beautiful mouth...

She was lost for words, and something about his expression made her think that it was the same for him, too.

It felt odd to have a ring sitting on her finger again. Odd, but strangely comforting.

They walked hand in hand through the gardens. Their first stroll as an engaged couple. And tomorrow they'd be married.

She pushed the nerves away. 'I love tulips,' she said. 'Especially those gorgeous red ones.'

'I know.' He smiled. 'You said so the night I cooked for you.'

She was surprised but delighted that he'd remembered.

'That reminds me, I haven't organised your bouquet,' he said. 'Would you like tulips?'

'Are we allowed to have a bouquet in the Clerk's Office?'

'Of course,' he said.

'Then red tulips would be nice,' she agreed.

'I'll arrange it. And I guess we ought to go and find your dress.' He paused. 'I do have an official photographer arranged for tomorrow. I hope you don't mind.'

'And they're the photos we're going to use to tell everyone?' she asked.

'Sort of. When we get back to London, I thought we could tell your family in person and mine by video call.'

'OK.' She took a deep breath.

'It's going to be fine.' He stroked her cheek. 'Actually, I couldn't have found anyone nicer to be married to.'

Did that mean he wanted to make the marriage real? Or were they both getting carried away by the romance of their 'elopement'? Because here in middle of Central Park, an oasis of calm in one of the busiest cities in the world, it was starting to feel like a fairy tale.

The horse-drawn carriage took them back to the limo, and Luc asked the limo driver to take them to the best bridal shop on Fifth Avenue.

'It's unusual for a guy to come shopping with his bride for a dress,' the shop assistant said once she'd greeted them and they'd explained what they wanted.

'It's not a traditional wedding—we're eloping,' Luc explained. 'We came here for a few days and I guess the place swept us both a bit off our feet. We got a marriage licence this morning, and we're getting married tomorrow in Manhattan.'

'How romantic!' The sales assistant smiled. 'And your accent tells me you're from England.'

'London,' Kelly said swiftly, not wanting to complicate things. 'We're doctors.'

'What sort of doctors?' the assistant asked.

'Heart surgeon and cardiologist,' Luc said.

The assistant clapped her hands together. 'Two heart doctors—well, isn't that cute? So do you have any idea what sort of dress you'd like?'

'Not a traditional long wedding dress,' Kelly said. 'Something pretty and summery. No veil.'

'OK. I can do that. What's your bouquet like?'

'Very simple—an armful of glossy red tulips,' Luc said. 'Which I'm going to order right now while Kelly tries on dresses.'

'I can give you the number of a good florist,' the assistant said. 'And if you'll allow me to suggest a few ideas, Kelly…'

'I'm completely in your hands,' Kelly said with a smile.

Half an hour—and six dresses—later, Kelly was wearing a white silk knee-length shift dress with a sweetheart neckline and a lace overlay; the sleeves were pure lace. Thanks to some very quick and deft manoeuvring by the assistant, Kelly's hair was up in a simple chignon, and she was wearing red, strappy high-heeled shoes to match the tulips that would be in her bouquet.

'You look amazing,' the assistant said with a smile.

Kelly barely recognised the sophisticated woman in the mirror as herself.

In that dress and shoes, and with her hair like that, she looked exactly like a suitable bride for Prince Luciano.

Or would Luc Bianchi think she'd gone too far?

'Thank you so much for your help,' Kelly said.

'My pleasure, sweetheart. I love dressing brides.' The assistant grinned. 'Especially ones with cute accents.'

'I'd better check that Luc likes the dress before I say yes.'

The assistant shook her head. 'It's bad luck for him to see the dress beforehand. And besides, I think he'll love it. He clearly adores you. I think it's so romantic that you came out here for a romantic time together and now you're actually getting married, just the two of you.'

And Luc's security team, who just happened to be browsing in the store, but Kelly didn't say that.

She changed back into her normal clothes and joined Luc outside.

'Everything OK?' he asked.

'Fine, thanks,' Kelly said with a smile. 'I have the perfect outfit.'

'And you, sir—I assume you have a suit?' the assistant asked when she'd boxed up Kelly's dress and shoes.

'I do,' Luc confirmed. 'It's a formal dark grey lounge suit.'

'With an ordinary shirt and tie? You know,' the assistant said thoughtfully, 'since this isn't a traditional wedding, you could get away with wearing something a little less traditional. Like losing the suit jacket, wearing a waistcoat instead, and adding a bow tie to match the bride's bouquet and shoes. It'd look amazing in photographs. Especially if your photographer shoots everything in black and white and then colours in just the red.'

Kelly and Luc looked at each other.

'Less traditional and less formal—I'm in,' he said with a grin. 'And you have an excellent eye for detail. Thank you.'

The assistant grinned back and found him a wing-tip white shirt, a red silk bow tie and a waistcoat that was grey silk at the back and red silk at the front. 'Have a wonderful time in New York. Happy wedding day for tomorrow—and every happiness for your future.' She hugged them both.

'Thank you,' Kelly said, hugging her back.

When they were back outside the shop, Luc looked at her. 'I think we should send her flowers.'

'Great idea,' Kelly said.

He smiled at her. 'We have the rings, the dress, the licence, and the bouquet is ordered— I think we have everything we need. What about your hair and make-up?'

She lifted one shoulder in a half-shrug. 'I can do all that myself.'

'I know it's not a traditional wedding,' Luc said, 'but that doesn't mean you should miss out on having a fuss made of you. I'll talk to the hotel and organise hair and make-up. And please don't argue; I'd like to do something nice for you.'

'Then thank you. That would be lovely.' She stifled a yawn. 'Sorry. I'm starting to flag a bit.'

Luc glanced at his watch. 'It'd be eleven at night, our time, and we had an early start; plus long-haul flights are tiring. How about we have an early dinner at the hotel and an early night tonight?'

'That sounds really good,' Kelly said gratefully.

She was almost too tired to enjoy the spectacle of the hotel's dining room, full of palm trees and pillars and with an amazing stained-glass dome, and she knew she wasn't appreciating how good the food was.

Luc kissed her goodnight in their parlour. 'I'm going to stay up for a bit, but I'll be quiet so I don't disturb you.'

'I can stay up a bit later with you,' she said.

He stroked her cheek. 'You look tired. Go to bed. I'll see you tomorrow. And prepare to be pampered in the morning.' He paused. 'Just out of interest—what's the neckline of your dress?'

'Sweetheart,' she said. 'I guess, since it's not a traditional wedding, you could see it now.'

'No. We'll stick with that particular tradition. I'm not going to see you now until the wedding. I'm going to have my breakfast with the guys tomorrow, and I'll have yours delivered by room service. The limo will take you to the Clerk's Office—I'll meet you there.'

And then, she thought with a shiver that was a mixture of excitement and nervousness, they'd get married...

CHAPTER EIGHT

THE NEXT MORNING, Kelly woke to find herself alone in the suite. Luc had left her two packages with a note propped up against them.

Another tradition—something 'old and borrowed', and something blue. See you at the Clerk's Office at two. L xx

She remembered the old rhyme. The new was obviously her dress and shoes. The 'blue' turned out to be a Tiffany box containing an exquisite pair of sapphire stud earrings.

But the 'old and borrowed' really made her catch her breath: a beautiful and clearly antique string of pearls. Another note from Luc said,

These were my grandmother's, if you'd like to wear them today.

Meaning that he'd like her to wear them?

OK. She could do that. And he'd made it clear that they would be borrowed, which was fine by her.

By the time she'd showered and dressed, room service arrived with her breakfast. And then she had an appointment at the beauty salon: a massage to relax her followed by having her hair and nails done. She had a sandwich and fruit for lunch—beautifully presented and making her feel very spoiled—and finally the beautician did her make-up. Just as they finished, the Reception called to say that her flowers had arrived.

The bouquet was gorgeous: a simple posy of glossy red tulips that matched her shoes and Luc's tie and waistcoat, with matching red silk ribbon tied round the stems to make them easy to carry.

Back in her room, she changed into her dress and stared at herself in the mirror.

In less than an hour's time, she'd be Luc's wife. For a few months.

Nerves fluttered in her stomach. But Luc was a good man, and she trusted him. Her family liked him. And what they were doing meant that Luc would be able to carry on with his career, making a real difference to the world, instead of being forced into a job that he'd hate. They were doing the right thing.

She brushed one finger along the pearls. 'Luc didn't tell me about you,' she said, 'but I'm guessing you were special to him, if he wants me to wear your pearls. I hope you know that I'll support your grandson through this whole thing.' She dragged in a breath. 'And, Simon. I'll always love you. This isn't to disparage our wedding at all. I'm helping a friend, and he's helping me. And then we're going to move on with our lives. I won't forget you, but I'm also not going to live in seclusion, because I know you'd hate me to shut myself away from the world. I just want to wait until I'm ready.'

The Reception called to tell Kelly that the limo was ready whenever she needed it. She headed downstairs, and sat in the back looking out at the city as the driver took her through the streets of Manhattan. Towards Luc. Towards their wedding. Towards whatever the future held.

Luc took a deep breath as he waited outside the Clerk's Office in Manhattan. Five minutes until Kelly was due to arrive.

He knew she'd keep her word and turn up

for their marriage of convenience, but he felt as nervous as any real groom might feel.

'Are you sure about this, boss?' Gino asked.

'Yes. It will send a very clear message to my father.' Luc looked at Gino. 'So I don't expect you to risk your position by being the witness. I can ask the photographer to do that.'

'Ask someone you barely know? Are you kidding?' Gino frowned and shook his head. 'It will be my privilege to be your witness. Besides, I'm already an accessory.'

Luc clapped his hand on Gino's shoulder. 'True. And thank you. I assure you there won't be any consequences.'

'I don't care if there are,' Gino said. 'I like Kelly. A lot. And you've been much happier since she's been around.'

'We're friends. The marriage is in name only,' Luc reminded him.

'She likes you. And I think you like her, too.'

He did. He was aware that his feelings towards Kelly had grown and changed over the last few weeks. That he was starting to fall for her. But he didn't want to put any pressure on her. He knew she needed time to get over losing Simon. It wasn't fair to ask her for something she couldn't give, and besides any real emotional involvement would make their simple marriage of convenience way too complicated. 'The limo's here,' he said, more to distract himself than Gino.

And he caught his breath as the driver helped Kelly out of the car. She looked absolutely stunning. The dress was gorgeous, the flowers and her shoes were the perfect pop of colour, and she was wearing his grandmother's pearls.

'Hi,' he said when she walked towards him. And how odd that his voice had gone all croaky, his palms were sweaty and his heart rate was galloping. Kelly was his friend. This was going to be a marriage in name only. So why did this feel right now as if it was for real?

'Hi.' Her voice was all breathless and shy, too.

'You look lovely.' And he couldn't resist leaning forward and kissing her lightly.

She blushed. 'You look pretty good, too. And thank you for the loan of these.' She touched the pearls with a fingertip.

'Pleasure.' He smiled. 'My grandmother would have liked you very much.'

'Were you close to her?' Kelly asked.

He nodded. 'She was the one who persuaded my father to let me train as a doctor in the first place.'

'These,' she said, 'feel like a symbol of approval.'

'They are,' he said softly. 'Ready?'

'Ready,' she confirmed.

They walked into the Clerk's Office together and collected their number so they could wait to be called into one of the two chapels. Luc took a snap of them on his phone. 'For posterity,' he said.

'You look beautiful, Kelly,' Gino said.

'Thank you.' She smiled at him.

'This is Patty, our photographer,' Luc said when a woman came over to them. 'Patty, thank you for coming. This is Kelly.'

'Pleased to meet you, honey,' Patty said. 'Your dress is beautiful. And the colour co-ordination between you—that's good.'

'We were thinking,' Luc said, 'or, rather, the wonderful sales assistant at the bridal shop suggested, maybe you could process some of the photos in black and white—'

'—and pick out the accents in red?' Patty finished. 'Great idea.'

Patty took a few shots of them together, and then their number was called.

'This is it,' Luc said, feeling incredibly nervous. There was no going back now. And this was the right thing to do, he was sure.

The chapel was painted apricot and peach,

with a pink striped abstract painting next to the lectern. The officiant announced them, and they stood at the lectern in front of the clerk.

'Welcome, Luc and Kelly,' the officiant said. 'If there is anybody present who knows of any reason why these two people should not get married, please speak now.'

There was silence.

'Do you, Luc, solemnly declare to take Kelly as your lawful wedded wife?'

'Yes, I do,' Luc said.

'Do you promise to honour and cherish her for as long as you both shall live?'

'I do,' Luc agreed.

'As a symbol of your promise, please place the ring on her finger,' the officiant directed.

Luc did so, smiling at Kelly. Nothing about this part was fake. He'd honour her always.

'Do you, Kelly, solemnly declare to take Luc as your lawful wedded husband?' the officiant asked.

'Yes, I do.' Her voice was firm and clear.

'Do you promise to honour and cherish him for as long as you both shall live?'

'I do,' she affirmed.

'As a symbol of your promise, please place the ring on his finger.'

She slid the matching ring onto his finger.

Luc caught her gaze, and he could see how enormous her pupils were. So did she feel this strange, unsettling, meant-to-be feeling, too?

'And as much as you both have consented to be united together in matrimony and have exchanged your wedding vows in front of us all here today, by the power vested in me by the laws of the great state of New York, I now pronounce you husband and wife,' the officiant said.

And that was it.

They were married.

'Mr and Mrs Bianchi, congratulations on behalf of the state.' The officiant smiled at both of them, signed a piece of paper with a flourish, waited for them both to sign it along with Gino as the witness, and then gave them their official marriage registration.

'So this is it,' Luc whispered.

'We're married,' she whispered back.

'You may kiss the bride,' the officiant said.

Luc did so, intending it to be light and easy, but somehow he couldn't quite pull away from her. He was aware of everything about her: the sweetness of her scent, the warmth of her skin, the feel of her mouth against his.

When he finally broke the kiss, he felt thoroughly flustered. And she looked as if she felt exactly the same way.

Patty took a couple of photographs, and then Luc held Kelly's hand as they headed outside. Patty posed them outside the doorway, with the words 'New York State' above their heads. She took a shot of them smiling, another with them showing off their wedding rings, another of them kissing—and then she took the bouquet and gave it to Gino for safe keeping. 'A little prop,' she said with a grin, and gave them a banner which proclaimed 'just married' in capital letters, with a heart separating the words.

Luc laughed. 'Just about perfect for two cardiac doctors.'

They held up the banner and Patty took a shot, then another of them on the steps under the words 'Office of the City Clerk'.

'Iconic pictures,' she said thoughtfully when she collected the banner and returned the bouquet to Kelly. 'I know just the place.'

At her direction, the limo driver took them to Brooklyn Bridge Park. She took a few shots of Luc and Kelly by the river with the iconic skyline and Brooklyn Bridge behind them, and then she shepherded them towards the carousel. 'It's a hundred years old,' she said with a smile. 'I think this is perfect for you two.'

She posed them both on the horses and in

one of the chariots, taking photographs of them as they whirled round on the carousel.

'And that's a wrap,' she said with a smile. 'Thank you for being patient. I'll deliver the final photographs at your hotel before breakfast tomorrow morning, and email you the link to the downloads so your family and friends can see them when you get home and order any prints they choose.'

'Thank you.' Luc shook her hand warmly, and Kelly hugged her.

'So now the photographs are over,' Luc said when Patty had left, 'that means dinner and dancing. I have things booked, if that's all right with you?'

'It all sounds wonderful,' she said. 'It's my first time in New York, so everything is new for me and I've had an amazing time already. I loved the carousel.'

'Me, too,' he said. 'Can you walk in these shoes?'

'Yes.'

'Then let's take a stroll,' he said.

And somehow it felt natural to walk with his arm around her shoulders, talking and enjoying the views and taking snaps on their phone for her to send home. As if they really were married and enjoying their honeymoon.

The limo took them back to Manhattan

for a swish meal in a Michelin-starred restaurant. And it was an incredible space, with pale walls and classical architecture that reminded Luc of the ancient palazzos in Bordimiglia. The tables and chairs were all made of dark polished wood, the starched damask tablecloths were white, and in the middle of each table was a bowl of tulips—some red, some yellow, some pink and some a dramatic deep purple. The whole thing looked beautifully stylish.

'Tulips! Our wedding flowers. Did you ask for them especially?' Kelly asked.

'No,' he admitted. 'It's pure serendipity. But I did ask if they would swap the red meat options on the tasting menu for something else of your choice, and they agreed.'

'Thank you.'

The meal was exquisitely cooked and exquisitely plated, and each course was served with the perfect matched wine. After coffee, and the nicest petits fours Luc had ever eaten, the limo took them to a small, intimate jazz club.

'Would you dance with me...?' He paused. 'Are you still Dr Phillips, or will you be known as Dr Bianchi?' It was the one detail they hadn't discussed—and it was an important one.

'If I kept my name,' she said, 'it might look

suspicious, so I guess I'll be changing my name to yours.'

'Then will you dance with me, Dr Bianchi?'

'With pleasure, Mr Bianchi,' she said.

Kelly loved the little basement space, with the jazz trio playing old love songs and the singer crooning into an old-fashioned radio-type microphone.

'The perfect evening for an elopement,' she said. Even if it wasn't a real one.

As she'd pretty much expected, Luc was an excellent dancer with a good sense of rhythm, and he guided her expertly through the steps of the dances she didn't know, whisking her through foxtrots and quicksteps and a cha-cha-cha.

And then everything slowed right down and he held her really, really close for an old-fashioned rumba. Kelly found herself holding Luc just as tightly, their movements so tiny and slow that it was as if they were swaying, rather than moving across the dance floor.

She looked up at him and there was a slash of colour across his cheeks. His eyes were huge and his mouth was slightly parted. And she couldn't help reaching up and stealing a kiss.

'Kelly,' he whispered, and kissed her back.

The whole world melted away.

She had no idea how long they kissed, what was playing, who was near them. All she was aware of was Luc—the warmth of his body, the scent of his skin, the feel of his mouth against hers.

When he broke the kiss, they were both shaking.

'This isn't supposed to be happening,' he said.

'I know,' she said. It was a marriage in name only. The rules were simple. And yet things were changing. This whole thing felt like a fairy tale—a dream. 'It's our wedding day,' she whispered.

'Yes.' He kissed her again. 'My beautiful bride.'

In name only. Except right now that wasn't what she wanted. She wanted *him*.

The sensible side of her knew that this would be complicating things. That if she followed her heart right now, tomorrow would be awkward and full of difficult questions. But she'd spent the last two years hiding away, burying herself in work. Since Luc had come into her life, things had started to change. She'd enjoyed their dates and getting to know each other. He'd reminded her that life could still be fun—that you could be a serious doctor and dedicated to your work, but at the same time you could enjoy a show or sit on a merry-go-round or dance to the kind of music that heated your blood.

Life was short. You couldn't predict what was going to happen.

Tonight, would it be so bad to give in to the desire that pulsed through her veins?

'Kiss me,' she whispered.

And he did.

It's our wedding day.

This was supposed to be in name only.

He really shouldn't have brought her to the jazz club, where the music oozed sensuality and the dance steps made him aware of every move she made. He should take a step back right now. He should definitely not be kissing her.

Yet he couldn't resist her.

Not when her green eyes were huge, when her lips were parted, when her voice was all soft and she was asking him to kiss her.

They both regret this tomorrow. It was so far away from their deal.

But he couldn't stop himself.

He kissed her. Danced with her, hardly aware of the beat of the music because the beat of his blood was thrumming in his veins. Held her close. Wanting her.

Being with her made him feel different. Made him want things he'd trained himself not to want, because it wouldn't be fair to start a relationship and then change all the rules.

Yet that was what was happening right now. Here, on the dimly lit dance floor. On their wedding day. *Their wedding night.*

'Kelly,' he whispered. 'It's our wedding night.'

She stroked his face. 'I don't want to dance any more.'

He needed to do the right thing. 'I'll take you back to the hotel.'

'And stay with me?'

His heart skipped a beat—and another. 'Kelly…'

'As you said, it's our wedding night.'

And they were both sober. It wasn't alcohol making him dizzy, it was desire. Desire he could see matched in her eyes—or was he just seeing what he wanted to see?

'Kelly…' He was lost for words. Tongue-tied. At sixes and sevens.

'Luc.' She reached up and kissed him, and he was lost.

He took her hand and led her out of the club to the limo. They didn't talk on the way back to the hotel, but it wasn't an awkward silence. When they arrived at the hotel, Luc's fingers tightened around hers and he helped her out of the car. Federico shadowed them to the lift, and then it was just the two of them.

Kelly looked suddenly nervous. And Luc could guess exactly why. It was their wedding night. They were alone. And her doubts and common sense were clearly creeping back in.

He kissed her lightly. 'If you've changed your mind, I won't pressure you.'

'I've not changed my mind. Just… It scares me a bit,' she admitted.

'I know. This kind of scares me, too,' he said softly, and kissed her again.

That strange, dizzying feeling was back, and she made no protest when he picked her up and carried her across the threshold of the suite.

'Tradition?' she asked, her voice husky.

He set her back on her feet. 'Tradition.' And he wanted that feeling back, the way things had been at the club. Romantic and sensual, just the two of them in a bubble and tomorrow could take care of itself. 'Dance with me again.'

She nodded, and he flicked into the Internet on his phone to find some soft, slow music. When he opened his arms, she walked into them and swayed with him to the music. When he kissed her, she kissed him all the way back. And when he picked her up and carried her to his room, she made no protest...

The next morning, Kelly woke in Luc's arms. In Luc's bed.

Memories of the previous night came rushing back, and her cheeks flooded with colour. She couldn't even blame last night on drinking too much, because they hadn't. They'd drunk wine with their meal, but not massive amounts.

Last night had been because they'd both wanted it.

But would things be different today?

'Good morning,' he said.

'Good morning.' What was the etiquette in this sort of situation—when you woke up in the bed of the man you'd married in name only? She didn't have a clue. Right now she was going to take her lead from Luc.

'I know we didn't plan last night,' he said.

He could say that again. 'No.'

'And we're going to have to decide what happens now.'

'We could pretend it didn't happen,' she said.

'If that's what you want.' He paused. 'Or

maybe we could look at this another way. We're here for a couple more days. Maybe we could have this as a kind of time out. Make this a real honeymoon.'

And did that mean the start of a real marriage? She hadn't let herself think of that possibility. It wasn't part of their agreement. But she really liked the man she was getting to know. The physical attraction was there, too. Did he feel the same?

She wasn't a coward, so she asked, 'And when we get back to London?'

He looked at her. 'It could get complicated. In London, it would be sensible to stick to Plan A.'

'A marriage in name only.'

'A marriage in name only,' he agreed.

The sensible side of her knew he was right. If they let themselves get emotionally involved, it would start to get messy when they had their quiet divorce in a few months' time. Besides, while they were out here they needed to take some convincing photographs to make their families believe that they were in love and had got married in a rush—and being intimate with each other was the best way to make it look convincing. So they needed to keep the here and now separate from the future.

'A real honeymoon here,' she said, 'and Plan A when we're back in London. That works for me.'

He stroked her face. 'Thank you.'

Kelly still felt a little shy with him, but at the same time she was starting to be more confident. Room service brought them coffee and the photographs that Patty had dropped off.

'She's done a fantastic job,' Luc said. 'And our sales assistant was right about the monochrome photos with an accent.'

'They're perfect. We should send her one of these with the flowers,' Kelly said.

'Agreed.' He kissed her lightly. 'Give me five minutes to sort it out, and we can go down for breakfast.'

'OK.'

Funny, this time round she hadn't married for love. But the way she and Luc were looking at each other in the photographs was very, very convincing. Either Patty was a genius photographer, or she'd spotted something that Kelly and Luc hadn't quite admitted to themselves was there...

She shook herself. This wasn't a good idea. She couldn't fall for him. They didn't have a future.

'It's all arranged,' Luc said. 'Patty's going

to courier a photograph over to the florist, and everything will be there this morning.'

'Perfect,' Kelly said with a smile.

After breakfast, the limo took them to the Met. They spent the morning wandering around, enjoying the art, and then headed for the Cloisters which housed the Met's medieval art collection.

'This is gorgeous,' she said. 'Those arches make this feel like being in the middle of medieval Italy.'

'It reminds me of the old parts of Bordimiglia,' Luc agreed.

They wandered through the gardens hand in hand, and visited the famous Unicorn Tapestries. Then Luc glanced at his watch. 'We need an early dinner. Is Times Square OK with you?'

She smiled. 'I'm happy to go wherever you like.'

He'd booked a table at a small place where they served the nicest pizza she'd eaten outside of Italy.

'Ready for this?' he asked, looking pleased with himself.

'Ready for what?'

'A couple of minutes and you'll see for yourself,' he said, shepherding her down Broadway. He stopped outside a theatre.

She looked up to read the sign and blinked. 'No way. No *way* have you got tickets for *Hamilton*. It's booked up years in advance!'

'There are certain advantages,' he said, 'to the other side of my life.'

She shook her head. 'I can't believe this.'

'Believe it. Here's the proof.' He produced tickets from his pocket and smiled at her. 'I think we need a selfie.'

She threw her arms around him. 'Luc, you're amazing. I've wanted to see this show so much—and, even though Susie calls me the Ticket Whisperer, I couldn't get tickets for us. Now I'm seeing it. On Broadway. With you. It's a real dream come true.'

She posed for a selfie with him, making sure to get the tickets and the theatre's sign in the shot. Then she looked at the picture and noticed the time. 'Oh, it'll be gone midnight back home. I'll send this tomorrow so I don't wake anyone up.'

Just as he'd done with *Les Misérables*, Luc had organised a box. 'Better get the programmes,' he said. 'We need four.'

'Four?' Kelly was mystified.

'You'll find out why later.'

'Why can't you tell me now?'

'Because I'm annoying,' he said with a grin, refusing to enlighten her.

The musical was every bit as good as she'd hoped, and she loved every second of it. And then, after the show, he shepherded her down to a restricted area where they got to meet the cast. At that point, she realised why he wanted four programmes: because the cast signed one each for her mother, Susie and Angela as well as one for her.

'That was so nice of you, tonight,' she said when they were finally back at their hotel. 'You really didn't have to organise that.'

He shrugged. 'I thought you'd enjoy it—and that your mum, Susie and Angela would appreciate a souvenir you definitely wouldn't get elsewhere. And if you can let me know some appropriate dates, my press team will organise tickets for you all to go together in London.'

She smiled. 'That would be amazing. Thank you so much.'

The next morning, before breakfast, Kelly sent the photographs to her mum, sister and Angela.

All three texted straight back with messages along the lines of How awesome is that? Can't believe how lucky you are.

Not just me. Luc says he can organise tickets for us all in London, she texted back. Just let me know dates.

Five minutes later, she looked at her new husband. 'According to the barrage of texts I've just received, you're now officially the new hero of three women in London.'

He laughed. 'Let me know the dates and I'll organise it.'

They went sightseeing again, taking the ferry out to Ellis Island and went to see the Statue of Liberty; Kelly bought paperweights for her dad, her brother-in-law and Angela's husband. They spent the afternoon in the Museum of Natural History seeing the dinosaurs and got models for the twins, and Luc's nephew and niece. Finally they watched the sunset from the Empire State Building before heading out to dinner.

But better than all the sights was being with Luc. Something seemed to have shifted in their relationship, and she was seeing him differently. As a lover, not just as a colleague.

This was a dangerous game. Kelly knew they were going back to Plan A once they were back in England. But, for now, it was fun to dream.

On their last morning in New York, they headed back to the Clerk's Office to sort out the paperwork to authenticate their American wedding certificate in Europe with an

Apostille. And then it was time to go back to London.

'Time to tell everyone,' she said.

At the airport in New York, Kelly texted her parents.

About to catch flight. Can we come and see you tonight when we get back? Ask Susie, Nick and the boys, too, please.

Luc put his arms round her. 'Don't look so worried. Everything's going to be just fine.'

She hoped so. She really, really hoped so.

CHAPTER NINE

'So did you have a wonderful time in New York?' Caroline asked, hugging Kelly and Luc in turn.

'We did, Mum,' Kelly said. 'And we brought presents.'

'Dinosaurs!' Jacob and Oscar chorused in delight when they opened their parcels, and they disappeared to play some complicated game about pterodactyls and a T-Rex.

'Dad, Nick, we hope you like these,' Kelly said.

The men duly exclaimed over their Statutes of Liberty.

'Mum and Susie…' Kelly handed over the parcels with a grin.

'Oh, wow!' Susie hugged them both when she saw the signed programmes. 'That's amazing.'

'And the tickets are booked for next month, in London,' Luc added.

'That's so kind of you.' Susie and Caroline were all smiles.

Kelly's pulse felt as if it had doubled. 'Um, we also have some news.' She swallowed. 'While we were away…' Her throat dried, and so did the words.

'It was all my fault,' Luc said. 'I kind of got swept away by the romance of New York.'

'You got engaged?' Caroline asked.

'Um—not quite.' Kelly held out her left hand.

'Hang on. There are two rings on your finger. Are you trying to tell us you got *married*?' Susie demanded.

'It's my fault,' Luc said again. 'And I apologise. And we'll have a proper celebration with you now we're back in London.'

'You got married.' Caroline's voice was flat, and Kelly realised just how her mother was feeling. Hurt and pushed out—because Kelly hadn't confided in her. Because Kelly had resisted all the suitable men paraded in front of her, and then got married to someone her family had only met once.

'Mum, we never meant to hurt anyone,' she said.

'If the other side of my life got involved, everything would be stuffy and formal, and I didn't want to put Kelly under that sort of stress,' Luc said. 'We really didn't do it to leave anyone out or hurt anyone.'

'We just wanted to keep it low-key,' Kelly said.

Luc put his arm round Kelly. 'I know it's fast and we've only known each other for a couple of months. But I have a huge amount of respect for Kelly. She's a brilliant doctor and one of the nicest people I know.'

'What about love?' Robin asked softly. 'You haven't said anything about love.'

Kelly went very still. Was Luc going to lie?

He'd really miscalculated this. Kelly had warned him that her family would be hurt, but Luc had been so focused on proving a point to his father that he'd brushed her worries aside. He'd thought of how his own family would react, with coolness and all emotions buried. Which wasn't how Kelly's family was at all.

And now he had to fix this. The last thing he wanted to do was to cause a rift between Kelly and her family.

He knew what Robin wanted him to say. That yes, Luc loved his daughter.

But he and Kelly hadn't talked about their feelings. He was pretty sure Kelly wasn't in love with him. She liked him, yes, and the physical attraction between them had been obvious in New York. But love? They hadn't said the words. And it felt wrong to say them now.

What did he do?

If he said no, he'd hurt her family. If he said yes, he'd probably freak Kelly out. It was a tough line to walk; but he was used to having to juggle the two sides of his life. Used to diplomacy, even though he wasn't as good at it as his sisters were.

He chose his words carefully. 'As you can imagine, I grew up in a rather different world. One where you pretty much keep your emotions private. Love isn't something I'm comfortable talking about.'

'It's a simple enough question,' Caroline said, her voice very neutral—but Luc could see the worry in her eyes. 'Do you love Kelly or don't you?'

He could feel the tension in Kelly's frame. To make this convincing as a whirlwind relationship, he knew what he had to say. Yet, if he said it, would Kelly think he was an accomplished liar, someone she couldn't trust?

It all depended on how you defined love.

Friendship plus physical attraction: under that definition, he loved Kelly. And he'd kept his emotions in check for so long that he wasn't sure he knew what love felt like any more.

'Yes,' he said softly. And he increased the pressure of his arm very slightly round Kelly so she'd know that it was a yes he could explain, and *would* explain later.

Either he was lying to her family or he'd been lying to her—and she didn't think Luciano Bianchi was a liar.

They'd never talked about love. If he loved her, surely he would've said the words to her in private, not blurted them out in front of her family?

Then again, her parents had pretty much forced the issue. Whatever he said would be difficult. If he said no and admitted it was a marriage of convenience, all hell would break loose. He chose to say yes. So was this a white lie to make a family feel better about their elopement? Or did Luc actually mean it?

And what did that little squeeze of his arm actually mean? Was it his way of saying they'd talk later, or was he saying sorry he hadn't said the words before, or was he saying he was stuck and he didn't want to hurt anyone and he wasn't putting any pressure on her?

She didn't have a clue. And it left her own feelings in a complete tangle. How did she feel about him? It wasn't the same kind of relationship she'd had with Simon—but was this love?

She couldn't think straight. Could hardly breathe. Couldn't meet her family's eyes.

Had she just made the biggest mistake of her life?

'If you really love my sister,' Susie said, 'then I'm happy. I get why you wanted to keep it low-key.'

Because Kelly had had the big wedding, last time round.

'And all we want is to see you happy. To see you living again instead of just existing for nothing except work. And I've seen the change Luc's made in you. Those photos you sent us from New York, with the two of you on Broadway—you looked so happy. Happier than I've seen you in two years,' Susie continued.

'So you're not angry with us?' Kelly asked.

'I think,' Robin said, 'we're sad we didn't get the chance to share it with you and throw confetti and drink champagne and dance very, very badly to the terrible music you girls all love.'

'But if you're happy, that means the world to us,' Caroline said.

'I'm sorry again,' Luc said. 'Maybe we can have a private celebration.'

'Just the family? That would be nice,' Nick said.

'A barbecue,' Robin said.

'Done. My place,' Luc said.

'Which I assume is where you're going to be living, now, Kelly?' Robin asked.

She nodded. 'Maybe we can do the celebration stuff next weekend.'

'Perfect,' Susie said. 'And please tell us you have *some* photographs from the wedding, even if they're selfies on your phone.'

'You have to wait for twenty-four hours between getting your licence and getting married,' Luc said, 'so I managed to book a photographer. I can give you the download link if you'd like to see them.'

'If?' Susie said, raising her eyebrows at him. 'Of course we want to see them.

'And, um, I have champagne in the car. Maybe we can have a toast while we look at the photographs. And obviously I'll order any prints you'd like,' he added. 'I know it doesn't make up for you not being there, but we really did want it to be low-key.'

'Champagne is an excellent idea,' Caroline said.

Luc fetched it swiftly, and Robin led the toast. 'To Kelly and Luc. Wishing you every happiness.'

'Every happiness,' the others echoed.

Everyone seemed to enjoy the wedding photographs. 'I love this one on the carousel,' Susie said softly. 'You look happy. It's so good to see the light back in your eyes.'

'I wish you'd been there,' Kelly said, hugging her. 'But if we'd both had our families there...'

'It wouldn't have been low-key any more,' Susie finished. 'Just as long as you're happy.'

'Have you told your own family yet, Luc?' Robin asked.

'No.'

'As the heir to the throne, you've deprived your country as well as your family of your wedding,' Caroline said quietly.

'They've already had my sisters' weddings,' he said. 'And Kelly's right—my life is complicated. I see myself as a doctor, not a king. I'm not the oldest child, and I think my older sister—who would make a fantastic queen and a much better ruler than I would—should be the one to take over from my father. It's utterly ridiculous that one chromosome should make so much difference, in this day and age,' he added, his words heartfelt.

'I agree with that,' Susie said. 'Though I think your family might be upset.'

His parents certainly wouldn't react with the warmth and openness of Kelly's parents, Luc thought. Maybe he could learn from Kelly how to make that particular relationship a little easier and less formal.

'So are you a princess now, Kelly?' Robin asked.

'No. As with your royal family, only someone of royal blood can be called a prince or princess after marrying into the royal family,' Luc answered. 'My father does have the right to bestow a title, if he chooses.'

'But that's not why I married Luc. I'm still Dr Kelly, the way I always was,' Kelly said. 'Although I'm Dr Bianchi now.'

'Still our Kelly,' Caroline said. She looked at Luc. 'Welcome to the family.'

'Thank you.' Awkwardly, Luc took his arm from round Kelly's shoulders and went to shake Caroline's hand.

She hugged him. So did Robin, Nick and Susie. 'Welcome to the family.'

Back in the car, Luc sighed. 'I'm sorry for hurting your family, Kelly.'

'They've forgiven us—now they're over the initial shock, they just want us to be happy,' she said. 'But I think your family will give you a harder time than mine.'

'We'll cross that bridge when we come to it.' He raised her hand to his mouth and kissed it.

'You told my family that you loved me.'

He knew she'd bring that up. 'If you define love as friendship plus physical attraction, then yes, I love you. I wasn't lying.'

'That's a very clinical way of putting it.'

Especially when those three little words had been said to her by her previous husband, and he'd meant that she was the love of his life. Guilt flooded through him. 'Most of the time, I have to keep my emotions under wraps. I'm expected to behave with quiet dignity,' he pointed out.

'Eloping to New York is hardly quiet dignity.'

'I know. But it was my idea, so I'm taking the blame.'

'It wasn't just you. I could have said no.'

'Thank you,' he said, 'for saying yes. And for being so supportive.'

'I said I'd help you.'

'But it's caused a row with your family— or as near a row as I guess you get to, given how nice they all are—and I really am sorry for that.'

'They'll come round,' Kelly said. 'Your family, on the other hand, might disown you for what we've done.'

He shrugged. 'Isn't there a famous quote,

"never trouble trouble till trouble troubles you"?'

'Yes,' she said wryly, 'but I have a nasty feeling you might have troubled trouble.'

Back at Luc's house, they went into his study together.

'Here goes,' he said. He switched on his laptop and video-called his parents.

There was a quick exchange in Italian that Kelly couldn't follow, and then Luc said, 'Can we speak English, please, Mamma?'

'English?'

'I'd like you to meet someone,' he said. 'Kelly, this is my mother, Vittoria. Mamma, this is Kelly.'

'Pleased to meet you, Your Majesty,' Kelly said, wishing she'd thought to ask Luc about etiquette before he'd called home.

'And you, my dear,' Vittoria said.

'Is Babbo around?' Luc asked.

'He's in Rome on business. Why?'

Luc coughed. 'I have some news. Kelly and I work together. She's a cardiologist. And we went to New York this week together.'

'I see,' Vittoria said.

Kelly didn't have a clue what Luc's mother was feeling. Now she understood what he meant about keeping his emotion under wraps. Quiet dignity definitely summed up his mother. Quiet *enigmatic* dignity.

'While we were there, we got married,' Luc said.

'Married.' Again, that quiet, measured, completely inscrutable tone. 'I see. And you want me to tell your father?'

'No—I'll do that. But I wanted you to be the first to know.'

'I see.'

Her own family had been upset at first. Kelly didn't have the faintest idea how his mother was feeling, right now. Horrified? Disapproving? Angry? Hurt? Without a clue how the other woman was feeling, she had no way of reassuring her or making things better. But she wanted to say something to support Luc. 'Luc's a good man. An excellent surgeon.'

'Indeed. He's also the heir to the throne of Bordimiglia,' Vittoria said.

'You know how I feel about that, Mamma,' he said.

'Indeed. You know how your father feels, too.' Vittoria paused. 'Did it not occur to you to introduce us before you got engaged, let alone married? It's very discourteous to your wife.'

Kelly really hadn't expected that, and it

made her feel even more guilty. 'It was discourteous to *you*, too, and I apologise for that.'

'I think I know whose idea it was to get married in a rush, child,' Vittoria said. 'We will speak later, Luciano.' And the screen went black.

Luc blew out a breath. 'That went relatively well.'

Was he kidding? She stared at him in disbelief. His mother had just hung up on him! How on earth could he think it had gone well? She'd be devastated if her mum had hung up on her.

'Babbo's on business, so I can't just call him. I'm going to leave him a voicemail asking him to call me before he speaks to Mamma.' He sighed. 'Things might get a little sticky over the next day or two.'

'Even though I didn't make any vows about for better or worse,' Kelly said, 'I'm your wife and I'll stand by you.'

'Thank you.' He closed his eyes for a moment. 'I kind of wish we were back in New York.'

'Rewinding time so we didn't get married in the first place?'

'No. I wish we were still on honeymoon. You and me, enjoying the sights of New York with the rest of the world a million miles away.'

On impulse, she wrapped her arms around him. 'We'll weather the storm.'

'Eventually.' He dropped a kiss on the top of her head. 'I shouldn't ask you this, but you haven't chosen your room yet. Would you stay with me tonight?'

Hold him until they both fell asleep? Common sense dictated that she should find an excuse; they'd both agreed that London would mean a return to Plan A rather than the closeness they'd shared in New York. But she wasn't going to push him away when he needed her. And right now she needed the comfort of his arms around her, too. 'We've had a long day. Yes.'

He kissed her lightly. 'I'll call my father. I guess I'd better talk to my sisters, too. If Mamma hasn't already done that.'

'I'll be here. Even if my Italian is currently limited to yes, no, hello, goodbye, please and thank you, I can at least be polite.'

'You,' he said softly, 'are an amazing woman.'

He left a swift message on his father's voicemail, and called his sisters. When he'd finished explaining the situation to them, his mobile phone rang.

'It's my father,' he said as he looked at the screen. 'I'd better take this.' Again, the entire conversation was conducted in rapid Italian, and Kelly felt very much surplus to requirements. She had absolutely no idea from Luc's expression how the conversation was going. But eventually he hung up.

'How did they take the news?' she asked.

'My father said we'll talk after he gets back from Rome. My sisters both say I'm an idiot but they'd like to meet you—sooner, rather than later.'

'Did you tell them it's a marriage of convenience?'

'No. They need to think it's real.'

'I'll do my best,' Kelly said. 'But I'm a cardiologist, not an actress.'

'And all this is well above and beyond the call of what I asked you to do. I really didn't expect it to get this complicated,' he said.

'Me, neither. But it's done now. We'll make the best of it.'

He held her close. 'I'm not sure I'd be quite as understanding if our positions were reversed.'

'Actually, I think you would,' she said.

She curled into his arms that night, and his lovemaking was so sweet and tender that it brought tears to her eyes. The next morning, they headed to her flat and packed all her belongings ready for the removal van. But when they returned to Luc's house, visitors were waiting for them.

Even before Luc spoke, Kelly could see the family resemblance and knew exactly who they were.

'Elle! Giu! I didn't expect to see you,' he said, sounding shocked.

His older sister rolled her eyes, hugged him and cuffed his arm. 'You are in *so* much trouble.'

'Getting married without your family. It's mean to leave us out,' his younger sister agreed.

He blew out a breath. 'That wasn't the intention. Did Mamma send you?'

'No. It was my idea,' Elle said. 'And we haven't seen you for ages.'

He winced. 'I'm sorry. That's my fault. I do love you all.'

'But you're focused on being a doctor,' Giulia said. 'We know.'

'Nice to meet you, Kelly,' Eleonora said. 'Now, Luc, go and do something while Giu and I get to know our new sister-in-law.'

'I'm not leaving her alone with you for you to grill her,' Luc said.

'Something to hide, brother dearest?' Giulia asked sweetly.

'No,' Kelly and Luc said simultaneously.

Eleonora and Giulia raised their eyebrows at each other.

'That's too swift a denial. They're definitely hiding something,' Elle agreed.

'We're not. We fell in love and we couldn't wait to get married. I sent you the wedding photographs,' Luc said. 'So you can see for yourself.'

His sisters shook their heads. 'You're almost Pinocchio, Luc. Your nose twitches when you lie,' Giulia said.

'It does not.'

'Oh, but it does. We have a theory,' Elle said casually, 'that you might have got married to someone unsuitable just to prove to our parents that you're unsuited to be King and Babbo should disinherit you.'

Luc's hand tightened round Kelly's, warning her not to react.

'Except we saw the press office report, Kelly,' Giulia said. 'And there's nothing remotely unsuitable about you. If you'd been a party girl who'd been in rehab a couple of times, or you had a brother who was in and out of jail, or something else that would make a lot of work for the palace PR team, Luc might have got away with it. But you're not quite what we expected.'

'We're in love,' Luc insisted.

'Also not true, because you would've told us and got us on your side to help talk Babbo round to the idea of you marrying someone who wasn't royal. So, basically, you're busted and you might as well tell us the truth,' Elle said.

'You're right,' Kelly said to Luc. 'She'd be a brilliant ruler. She's scary.'

'That comes from having two children under the age of five,' Giulia said. 'It makes you develop the scary mum radar. So are you going to tell us the truth?'

Luc raked a hand through his hair. 'I'm the heir. I'm pulling rank.'

Elle scoffed. 'No. You're going to make coffee, because we gave Maria the rest of the day off.'

'Better idea. I'll make the coffee and some choc-chip cookies to go with it,' Kelly said.

'Better idea still,' Giulia said. 'We'll come with you and make cookies, and Luc can go and do blokey stuff.'

'Bu—'

'We're going to have a girly chat. It might involve the menstrual cycle,' Giulia said.

Luc laughed. 'I'm a doctor. I don't get embarrassed that easily. You can talk about menstruation. I might even be able to give you some good advice.'

'Luc, just go and do something useful,' Elle said. 'We want to talk to Kelly.'

'No interrogation,' Luc warned.

Elle rolled her eyes. 'As if we'd interrogate someone who's just promised to make us cookies.'

'Susie grilled you. I'd expect nothing less,' Kelly said. But she also knew she'd have to be really careful about what she said.

'Cookies first,' Giulia said.

'In *my* kitchen,' Luc said plaintively.

'*Ciao*, Lukey. You don't have enough X chromosomes to join us,' Elle said, and together she and Giulia swept Kelly into the kitchen.

Luc's sisters kept everything light until the cookies were out of the oven. Then Eleonora made a pot of coffee.

'Right. We already worked out why he married you—you're a cardiologist, and marrying you shows Babbo how committed Luc is to his job, because he's chosen a partner in the same line of work.' She looked at Kelly. 'But what do you get out of marrying him? It's clear you're not a gold-digger.'

Kelly remembered how Luc had defined love, last night: physical attraction plus friendship. That worked for her, too. 'I love him,' she said.

Eleonora looked at her. 'You've known each other for how long?'

'Nearly two months. We met when he first came to work at the Muswell Hill Memorial Hospital,' Kelly said. 'Sanjay—our boss—asked me to show him round. And then we kind of fell for each other.' Sticking to the truth as much as possible would mean less chance of slipping up.

'You're a widow,' Giulia said.

Clearly she'd read the files on Kelly. Kelly nodded.

'I'm sorry you lost your husband.'

'Thank you.'

'You must have loved him very much,' Elle said.

'I did.'

'Two years. It's a long time to be alone,' Giulia said.

'My friends and family felt it was time for me to move on.'

'What about you?' Elle asked. 'How did you feel about it?'

'Not ready,' Kelly admitted. 'But then I met Luc.' And that was true. Since their 'honeymoon', they'd grown closer. A lot closer. To the point where they hadn't quite gone back to being sensible.

'So has your family met Luc? Or are you keeping this secret from them?' Giulia asked.

'They've met him,' Kelly said. 'They liked him. But we didn't tell them about the wedding until last night, when we came back from New York.'

'How upset were they?' Elle asked.

'They were upset at first,' Kelly admitted. 'And we both feel bad about that. But they understood why we wanted to keep everything low-key. I'm sorry if we've upset everyone in your family. That wasn't the intention.'

'Luc's idea, was it?' Giulia asked.

'It was the least complicated option,' Kelly said. 'Except now I'm wondering if we should have told everyone first.'

'Mamma is doing her Serene Swan bit and Babbo is frothing at the mouth,' Giulia said.

'I'm sorry,' Kelly said again. 'But I know how much Luc loves his job. And he's really good at what he does. I sat in on some of his operations and he's amazing to watch. He's already made a difference to our department— he's brought in new ideas and new training. He's wonderful with patients and he even gives up his breaks to sit and reassure nervous patients. And he's great with junior staff. He's helping to train the surgeons of the future. That's really important. And he wants to open a state-of-the-art cardiac unit in Bordimiglia in a couple of years' time.'

'But all his life he's known that he was born to take over from my father,' Elle said gently.

'And he's protested about it,' Kelly said. 'I believe your grandmother persuaded your father to let Luc go to medical school.'

'She did,' Giulia said.

'And you, Elle, are already doing some of your father's job—and Luc says you're excellent. That you would make a much better ruler than he would. I trust his clinical judgement absolutely and I trust his judgement outside work.'

'Even the elopement?' Giulia asked.

Kelly winced. 'We thought we were doing the right thing.' She looked Elle in the eyes. 'Do you think he'd make a better job than you would of running the country?'

'No,' Elle said.

'So,' Kelly said, 'we agree on that. Giulia, do you think Elle would be a better ruler than Luc?'

'Yes,' Giulia said.

'Then the way forward is obvious. I want to help Luc to follow his dreams and set up that cardiac centre,' Kelly said. 'I believe in him.'

'So do we,' Elle said.

'I'm assuming your parents sent you to

check me out,' Kelly said. 'So what are you going to tell them?'

'That you're a doctor,' Elle said. 'That you're nice. That you believe in Luc.' She paused. 'But I do think Luc rushed into this— and that's probably my fault, for telling him that Babbo has been talking about stepping down next year. It panicked Luc into making a rash decision.'

'So you think he shouldn't have married me?'

'Not this quickly,' Elle said. 'He hasn't given you a chance to see the other side of his world. You might find it too much to deal with.'

'Like Rachel?' Kelly asked.

Giulia looked surprised. 'He told you about that?'

Kelly nodded. 'I know he's been hurt before. And I would never hurt him.'

'I believe you,' Elle said.

'So will you support Luc?' Kelly asked.

Elle spread her hands. 'Right now I could happily punch him for being so impetuous and causing a row with our parents, but we all know his heart lies in medicine. Taking him away from that would be like ripping his soul out. He'd do his duty if he had to, I know. But I wouldn't force him to do that.'

'So where do we go from here? And what can I do to help?' Kelly asked.

'I think, just be yourself,' Giulia said. 'Our parents will calm down—as I'm sure your family will, too. We'll get to know each other.'

'But I'm satisfied that you care about my brother,' Elle said. 'You're fighting his corner. And that's what I want for Lukey. Someone who'll back him but who'll also see when you need to compromise and talk him round from being stubborn.'

'Thank you.' Kelly hugged them both. 'Luc loves you. He talks about you with a great deal of affection and respect.'

'We love him, too,' Elle said. 'So we'll work on Babbo and make him think about the situation.'

'Hopefully he'll think it's his idea to change things the way Luc wants. The way we all want it, really,' Giulia said.

Elle smiled. 'Welcome to the family.'

CHAPTER TEN

EARLY ON SUNDAY MORNING, Kelly's mobile shrilled. She checked the screen, then answered swiftly. 'Susie? What's wrong?' she asked. 'Are the boys OK? Mum and Dad? Nick?'

'It's not us,' Susie said. 'It's the news. Someone sent your wedding photo to the press.'

'Luc's family knows. His sisters are staying with us right now,' Kelly said.

'It's not that, either. Kel, you need to talk to his press people. It's what they're saying about you.' Susie gulped. 'About Simon. How he died from heart disease and you're a cardiologist.'

Kelly felt sick. The very thing she wasn't able to forgive herself for. They'd homed straight in on it. And it wasn't just her who'd be hurt by this—it would be her family and Simon's family, too. 'Do Mum and Dad know?'

'Not yet. I'll tell them,' Susie said. 'But you

need Luc's PR team to jump on it now. There's no way you're to blame for Simon's death, and you know it.'

Kelly dragged in a breath. 'I'd better call Jake, too. And I'll call you back to let you know what's going on.'

She flicked into the Internet on her phone, and the sick feeling increased. According to the news, 'Dr Death'—meaning Kelly—married Prince Luciano in secret. And there was the picture of them outside the Clerk's Office in Manhattan. Looking into each other's eyes and laughing. How on earth had the press got hold of this? And where did they even begin to untangle this mess?

She knew Luc would be in the gym, where he worked out every morning with his security team. She showered and dressed swiftly, then went in search of him.

'What's wrong?' Luc asked, putting down the barbell he'd been working with.

She opened her mouth to tell him, and to her horror all that came out were racking sobs.

'Kelly?'

She held her phone out to him.

He read the story and wrapped his arms around her. 'I'm so, so sorry. I never thought they'd stoop this low. I'll get in touch with the PR team and get them to ask for a retraction.'

'They're calling me "Dr Death".' And how that description hurt.

'That's rubbish, and you know it. Think how many lives you've saved.'

'My patients—if they see this, they'll worry I'm not treating them properly, and the stress could trigger a full-blown CV event.'

'Anyone who's been treated by you will know how thorough you are and that this is utter rubbish,' he reassured her. 'I'll sort this. Go and grab some coffee, and I'll talk to my press team, Sanjay and the hospital press team.'

'I need to ring Simon's family. I never told them I got married to you.'

'Call them, and if they want to talk to me that's fine.' He held her close. 'Don't worry. We'll fix this. I'll get Elle and Giu.'

'Your family is going to hate me.'

'No, they're not. Elle and Giu will know immediately that this is all rubbish. So will my parents.' He hugged her again. 'We'll fix this. Call Jake and make a coffee.'

It was one of the most horrible conversations she'd ever had. Jake reassured her that he and the rest of his family knew she wasn't to blame for his brother's death—and she was the one who had made him and Summer get checked out. But she still hated herself.

'Congratulations on the wedding, Kelly. I hope you'll be happy,' Jake said. 'Simon wouldn't have wanted you to be alone.'

'Thank you,' she said, feeling guilty about lying to someone else. 'And I'm sorry. I should've told you that I was seeing someone instead of letting you hear about it in the press.'

'We're not on his trial because of you, are we?' he asked.

'No. I asked him if he'd consider you, yes, but you met the requirements or you wouldn't have been accepted,' she said.

She called Simon's parents next, feeling the same flood of guilt about not forewarning them. By the time she finished, Eleonora and Giulia had joined her in the kitchen.

'Toast. Eat,' Giulia demanded, putting a plate in front of her.

'I can't.'

'You can and you will. The press can be vile. But none of this is your fault,' Giulia said.

'I'm so sorry,' Kelly whispered. 'It's made trouble for your family.'

'That doesn't matter. We're used to the press. You're not,' Eleonora said. 'We'll remind them of the laws of defamation and get your name cleared.'

'How did they even know we'd got married?' Kelly asked.

'You sent the picture to the woman who sorted out your wedding dress. One of her colleagues saw it and recognised Luc—she's a big fan of European royal families—and she leaked the news to the press,' Eleonora said. 'And they started digging for information about you. Unfortunately they decided to spin it a nasty way.'

'That's so unfair to Simon's family,' Kelly said.

'And it's grossly unfair to you, sweetie. Give it an hour and they'll be singing a different tune,' Giulia said.

Luc walked back into the kitchen. 'The castle press team is already on it—they picked it up earlier but I didn't see their messages. I've given a statement. Sanjay sends his best and says not to worry, Kelly—we're all behind you on this. Though you and I are in a tiny bit of trouble with the department for sneaking off and getting married without telling them. We need to turn up with cake tomorrow.'

'We can make cake,' Eleonora said. 'And you need to talk to our parents.'

'I've already done that,' Luc said. 'Mamma was very definite about this being another good reason to get married properly instead of eloping. And that I don't have the sense I was born with. And that I need to look after my wife more carefully.'

'She doesn't hate me for dragging your family's name through the mud?' Kelly asked.

'You haven't. It's not your fault. It's probably a slow news week,' Giulia said. 'Mamma doesn't hate you. She's not happy about the secret wedding, but she's looking forward to meeting you.'

'We need to make sure your family is protected, too,' Eleonora said. 'We should have everything cleared up today, but maybe they'd like to come and spend the day here, just in case anyone decides to doorstep them.'

'I'll arrange it,' Luc said. 'Elle, Kelly has two nephews around the same age as Alessio and Anna.'

'I'll call Riccardo and get him to bring them over. The flight's only a couple of hours.' She frowned. 'Babbo's meant to be in Paris. We might be able to get him and Mamma over. But if they can't make it then the others will be here. And what better way to show the press that our families are united than to have a family party?'

Before Kelly knew quite what was going on, it was all arranged. As Eleonora had said, King Umberto and Queen Vittoria were due in Paris and couldn't move their schedule, but Eleonora's husband and children and Giulia's husband would be there.

Luc was smiling as he told them, 'Kelly, your dad is dying to practise his barbecue skills. I suggested everyone should bring their swimming things, so between us we can keep all the children amused. And you and I are going to take cake and bubbles to the paps.'

'We're facing them down?' Kelly almost squeaked.

'We're charming them into seeing the truth.' Luc looked at Eleonora. 'I don't suppose you can tell Ric to bring your best tiara?'

'No,' Eleonora said, rolling her eyes at him. 'But yes to playing nice with the paps. Kelly, your father and I can join you as our family representatives, if you wish. And I'm sorry you've had such a baptism of fire.' She patted Kelly's shoulder. 'Now, we have cake to make.'

This was surreal, Kelly thought, making cake in the kitchen with two princesses. But Eleonora and Giulia were down-to-earth, and by the time her family arrived she was a lot more relaxed. She introduced them all swiftly, and the women all bonded over making desserts and salads, while the men played with the children in the garden and sorted out the barbecue.

'Do we call you "Your Highness" or "Your Majesty"?' Susie asked Eleonora.

'Neither. You're family, so we stick with first names,' Eleonora said. 'Call me Elle.'

When Eleonora's children arrived, it took all of five minutes for the children to become firm friends. Kelly's new brothers-in-law were relaxed and charming.

'You learn to grow a thick skin with the press,' Eduardo said. 'You can't please everyone, and everyone on social media has an opinion. Unless you really *are* behaving badly and deserve what they say about you, take what they say with a pinch of salt.'

'Though in this case they're being unfair,' Riccardo said. 'So the press team will jump on them and put them straight. You'll get an apology tomorrow.'

'Today would be better,' Luc said. 'And I think Kelly and I have a delivery to make.'

The photographers and journalists hanging round the far side of the gate on Luc's road all seemed shocked at having cake, champagne and chilled sparkling water served to them by a prince.

'Kelly's family and mine are celebrating our good news,' Luc said, 'and we thought you might like some refreshments.'

'That's nice of you,' one of the photographers said.

'We eloped to try to get out of the speeches and hours of photographs,' Luc said. 'Which kind of backfired. But my wife is an excellent cardiologist. I'm sure you'll all agree that if you're not experiencing any symptoms, you won't think there's anything wrong with you or that there's any need to see a doctor. And if it's the sort of condition that only gets picked up by having electrodes attached to your chest and being hooked up to a monitor, it can't possibly be diagnosed. There wasn't anything for Kelly to miss. Just so you're aware, the head of our cardiac unit has given a public statement saying exactly that.'

One or two of the journalists shuffled, looking guilty. 'Sorry.'

'I just hate to think that any of my patients have read the news and started getting worried about their own treatment. Stress isn't a good combination with a heart condition,' Kelly said.

'I don't think any of us thought about them,' one of the photographers admitted.

'You're all trying to sell newspapers and make a living,' Luc said. 'I get that. But a lot of people have been hurt needlessly by the story. Yes, we eloped, and it hasn't turned out to be the easy solution we thought it was going to be. But haven't any of you been swept away in the heat of the moment?'

'We all make mistakes,' one of the journalists said.

'Exactly. So enjoy cake and bubbles on us,' Luc said.

'Thank you, Your Highness. And we hope you're very happy together,' one of the other journalists said.

'Give us a kiss?' one of the photographers asked, holding up his camera.

Luc grinned. 'We're in the middle of a family party. We've been playing in the pool with all the kids and we're not exactly dressed up for an official photograph.'

'Just like any other family on an early summer Sunday afternoon when it's not raining,' the photographer said. 'Actually, our readers would love to know you're just like us.'

Luc and Kelly exchanged a glance, and did as they were asked, to a barrage of camera flashes and clicks.

And by the time they'd finished the barbecue, the photographs of that kiss were all over the news sites. Except this time the headlines said *The Surgeon To Mend Her Broken Heart*.

At the end of the afternoon, everyone crowded round Luc's piano while he played.

He deliberately chose the kind of songs that Kelly, her mum and her sister loved; and Kelly was thrilled that her new sisters-in-law joined in.

The only sticky moment was when Oscar spilled blackcurrant juice all over the white carpet. But Luc was completely unfazed. 'I've spilled coffee on this carpet before now. It will be fine. Stop worrying,' he said.

'It's absolutely true,' Giulia said. 'If anyone spilled things when we were growing up, it was always Luc. Don't worry.'

Eleonora was already in the kitchen, and returned with kitchen towel.

Between Eleonora, Kelly and Susie, they managed to get the stain out of the carpet. And while they were doing that, Giulia and Caroline made tea. 'The English solution to everything,' Giulia said. 'And it's definitely better here than it is anywhere else in the world...'

Later that night after everyone had gone home, Kelly curled in Luc's arms.

'I know that look,' he said. 'What are you thinking?'

'That today started horribly but the end was really nice. Our families get on.'

'Four children splashing around in the pool will make anyone laugh and get on,' he said.

'But you're right. Today was nice. Even though you panicked a bit too much over spills.'

Kelly paused. 'How today was—is that the kind of family thing you had, growing up?'

'My generation is a little less formal, as adults,' he said.

Which told her that his childhood had been much more restricted.

'It is how it is,' he said softly, as if guessing what she was thinking. 'I like this side of my life. The private side, where I'm a doctor rather than a prince.'

She just hoped that he'd get the chance to keep it that way.

'I've been in touch with Elle and Giu a little more often recently than I have been for a couple of years,' he said. 'And that's all thanks to you. Seeing you with your family has reminded me of what I'm missing.'

'I'm glad you're getting closer to them,' she said. 'I wouldn't be without my family.'

'And I wouldn't be without mine. Though I wish my father wasn't so stubborn.'

She stroked his face. 'And you don't think you might be a chip off the old block?'

'Probably.' He kissed her. 'But thank you. You're making my world a better place.'

'Good.' She kissed him back. 'Being a doctor doesn't mean you can't be close to your family. And maybe if you let your dad a bit closer, he might start to understand why you feel the way you do. And then you might be able to reach some sort of compromise.'

'I'm beginning to think,' Luc said, 'that women are much more diplomatic than men.'

'I don't know about that. The way you were with the press—I wouldn't have had a clue how to get them on my side. You made things better again.'

'Though if you'd never met me, you wouldn't have been in the press in the first place,' he pointed out.

'But you fixed it. That's the main thing.'

'My press team fixed it.'

'To your brief.' She paused. 'You might be a better king than you think you'd be.'

'Are you on my dad's side, now?'

'No. I'm just saying that maybe you need to look at things through his eyes. Work out a compromise together. Maybe there's a way you can work at your clinic but also carry out some royal duties as well—have the best of both worlds.'

'Maybe,' he said. 'Maybe.'

At work on Monday, Luc and Kelly went to see the head of the cardiac department before the start of their shift.

'I'm glad the papers have got the story right now,' Sanjay said. 'Are you all right, Kelly?'

She nodded. 'I'm just so sorry the hospital got dragged into this.'

'The press team are rushed off their feet giving tips and writing articles on heart health,' Sanjay said, 'so it's working out in the right way now.' He looked at them. 'Though you *are* in trouble about the wedding.'

'We brought cake,' Luc said, indicating the box he was carrying.

'Not good enough. I thought something might be going on, but I don't like rumours so I didn't ask.'

Kelly winced. 'Sorry.'

'Your private life is your affair—but you really can't get married without a proper cardiac department celebration,' Sanjay said.

'He's right. Dancing and toasting you in champagne. That's the very least you're getting away with,' Mandy, Sanjay's secretary said, coming in. 'I can't believe you two kept something like that quiet.'

Kelly and Luc exchanged a glance.

'I guess we kind of made everyone miss out on the wedding, so I'll get a reception organised,' Luc said. 'I'll ask my team to make the arrangements. Maybe we can do it instead of the next team night out?'

'A week on Friday. Good idea,' Sanjay said. 'Apart from all that stuff in the papers, I imagine your families aren't wonderfully happy about you eloping.'

'We didn't do it to hurt people,' Kelly said.

'You did it to avoid the fuss and the media circus. I understand that—though you rather got the media circus anyway,' Sanjay said. 'But we still want to celebrate your wedding with you. It's great news. Congratulations.'

The rest of their colleagues reacted in the same way, shocked by the way the news had broken and furious with the press on Kelly's behalf, a little hurt that they'd been kept in the dark about the wedding, but pleased for both of them.

Over the next week, they were rushed off their feet at the hospital. Luc worked on a rare domino transplant with two other surgical teams—a new heart and lungs for a patient who had cystic fibrosis, and then her healthy heart was transplanted to a patient with right ventricular dysplasia, a genetic disorder that caused a dangerously abnormal heart rhythm. After the operation, Luc was physically drained but mentally invigorated.

'I love the fact we can do this and give someone such great quality of life,' he said. 'It's only the second time I've worked on a domino transplant. The first team removed the heart-lung from the deceased donor, I transplanted them to my patient and removed her heart, and the third team implanted her heart into their patient.' He wrapped his arms around her. 'Normally, patients don't know anything about the donors or their families; but as they're being looked after in adjacent rooms I think there's a good chance they'll meet.'

'And your cystic fibrosis patient could hear her heart beating in someone else's body.' She paused. 'Something like this doesn't happen often. It'll be in the news.'

'I think the journalists will be a bit more sympathetic, this time round,' he said. 'Though the most important thing is that our patients are going to be able to walk down the corridor without having to stop and rest. As cystic fibrosis is a genetic condition, she'll still need treatment for it, but at least her new lungs will be working and not displacing her heart any more,' he added. 'She'll still need a lot of care, and there are the usual risks of organ rejection, infection and complications, but she'll have fewer symptoms and a better quality of life.' He looked at Kelly. 'I wish Babbo could understand how this feels. To be able to make a real difference to someone's life.'

'Maybe you should show him. Ask your patients if they'd mind doing a video interview with you so your father can see for himself,' she suggested. 'Explain it won't be shown to anyone else, and you'll delete it once your father's seen it.'

'That,' he said, 'is a brilliant idea.' He hugged her. 'And we have our wedding reception on Friday.'

'It's so good of Maria to make us an official wedding cake.'

'She's loving the fact that I put her in complete charge of the reception and gave her free rein to choose whatever she thought appropriate,' Luc said. He smiled. 'I hope everyone doesn't mind swapping the team bowling night out for dancing, a buffet and bubbles.'

'Given that we're inviting partners and children as well, everyone's happy,' she said. 'Though maybe we should have waited a little bit longer so your family could make it as well as mine.'

'We promised work we'd do it—besides, it's less complicated this way,' he said.

On Friday night, Gino drove them through Hampstead to a nearby stately home. Maria had arranged taxis for all the guests, and Luc and Kelly were the last to arrive.

They walked through a marble-floored hall with Venetian glass chandeliers hanging from the ceiling and massive paintings in gilt frames hanging on the wall.

'I feel a bit of a fraud,' Kelly whispered.

Luc's fingers tightened round hers. 'We're just giving everyone what they want to see—and a party. It's fine.' He smiled at her. 'And you look amazing, by the way.'

'So do you.' They'd decided to wear the same outfits they'd worn for the actual wedding, to make everyone feel that they were part of the day.

When they walked into the main hall, they could see the band set up at one end of the room, a generously laid out buffet table, and plenty of seating round the edges for guests. Music was playing through the sound system, but it stopped as soon as Luc and Kelly were in the room. Everyone turned to look at them, and then there was an eruption of party poppers and confetti.

'Speech,' someone called.

'And that,' Luc said with a grin, his voice booming over the crowd, 'is one of the best reasons ever for eloping. No long speeches to send everyone to sleep. I'll just say thank you all for coming, a special thank you to Maria for organising everything and making us a wonderful cake, and thank you to Maybe Baby for agreeing to be our band for the night. Enjoy yourselves, everyone.'

The party was in full swing and Luc and Kelly were dancing when a couple walked up to them.

'I think,' the man said, 'the next dance with the bride should be mine, given that she's my new daughter-in-law.'

'Babbo!' Luc hugged his father. 'I thought you and Mamma were on a state visit somewhere?'

'We explained that our wayward son was having a belated wedding reception,' his mother said. 'Since we were deprived of the wedding itself, we weren't going to miss the reception.' She smiled at Kelly to soften the edge of her words. 'I know whose idea it was to elope. Hopefully you can teach my son better manners than I did.'

'I—um—Your Majesties—' Kelly, completely flustered, was about to dip into a curtsy, when King Umberto took her hand. 'No formalities, child. This is my son's wedding party, so we will conduct it how he likes it—with no pomp or ceremony. But I would like this dance.'

'Yes, Your M—'

'Babbo will do,' the King cut in with a smile.

'And I look forward to meeting your family. Eleonora has told me all about them.'

'I—um—thank you,' Kelly said.

Once she'd danced with the King, she and Luc introduced his parents to her family. Although Umberto and Vittoria were more formal than their children, they did seem to be genuinely pleased to meet Kelly's family, and the introductions were easy.

'I had no idea they were going to be here,' Luc said.

'You're not the only one who can spring surprises, little brother,' a voice informed them.

'Elle!' He hugged his sister. 'I should have guessed you'd have something to do with it.'

'I've been looking forward to your second wedding reception—even though, being you, you gave us practically no notice.' Elle hugged Kelly. 'Cake, dancing and spending time with my favourite sister-in-law. What could be better?'

'I assume you're staying with us?' Luc asked.

Elle shook her head. 'Babbo arranged a hotel. But we'll be round to see you in force tomorrow for a proper family dinner party.'

'I was going to give Maria the weekend off.'

Elle grinned. 'Too late. She's already planned the menu and has everything ordered for delivery first thing tomorrow. And your family will be there too, Kelly.'

'They know about it?' Kelly asked.

'They know. Actually, Mamma had a long video call with Caroline earlier this week. Thankfully your mother is a little better with technology than mine.' Elle patted Kelly's shoulder. 'Just so you know, she thinks my brother made a good choice. Even if he went about it in an unconventional way.'

'I'm glad you're all here,' Luc said. 'I do love you all. Even if you think I'm an ungrateful brat.'

'Not a brat, and not exactly ungrateful. You just don't march to the same drum as Babbo,' Elle said.

The rest of the evening passed in a blur.

And then Keely, the paediatrician singer from the band, spoke up. 'We have a special guest tonight—you might not know he plays rhythm guitar as well as being a heart surgeon, but he does. Please give a round of applause for Luciano Bianchi.'

'How...?' Luc asked.

Elle gave an overdramatic shrug and spread her hands. 'No idea.'

'Of course you don't,' Luc said, rolling his eyes, and went onto the stage to join the band. Anton, the lead guitarist from the maternity department, handed him a guitar, and Luc joined the band for a couple of songs.

'I have it on good authority that he sings as well,' Keely said. 'And I think he should sing something for his new bride.'

Anton swapped Luc's guitar for an electro-acoustic, and Luc stared at Kelly.

Singing to his bride in public.

The woman he'd married in name only—except it wasn't quite turning out that way. She still hadn't moved into her own room at his house, and waking up with her in his arms was turning out to be the best part of his day. Despite their agreement, he was definitely falling in love with her. Everything about her, from her kindness to the way she sang in the shower to her infectious giggle.

But did she feel the same way about him? Was he just her transition partner, the one who would help her to move on from losing the love of her life? Or was this thing between them changing for her, too?

He was aware that everyone was waiting for him to play. And there was only one song he could think of. The one he'd sung to her, the first night she'd come to his house and they'd sat together at his piano.

The room felt huge; yet, at the same time,

it felt so small that he could hardly breathe. This was telling the world how he felt about her, singing a romantic song they'd expect to hear and yet not putting pressure on Kelly. Would she know that he was singing this for real—for her—or would she think that it was all part of their fake marriage?

His hands were shaking and he made a real mess of the introduction to the song. How could he mess up four simple chords like that? 'I can assure you I'm a better surgeon than I am a musician,' he said, making everyone laugh—including Kelly and his parents. And then he began the song again, holding Kelly's gaze and hoping that she knew what he was trying to tell her.

Everyone cheered when he'd finished. And then thankfully he was able to hand the guitar back to Anton and dance with his bride again.

'That was a beautiful song,' she said. 'The one you sang to me, that first night at your house.'

'Yes.' Pleased that she'd remembered, he stole a kiss.

At the end of the evening, Luc and Kelly said their goodbyes and headed back to his house.

'I guess,' he said, 'as that was our official wedding reception, I should do official groom stuff.' He picked her up and carried her over the threshold.

She kissed him before he set her back on her feet, so he carried her upstairs to their bed. And tonight felt the same as New York: just the two of them, and the rest of the world was a million miles away.

'Kelly,' he whispered.

'What?'

He was going to tell her he loved her—but then he chickened out. If he told her now, and she wasn't ready to hear it, he'd blow his chances of making their marriage a real one. 'Thank you for tonight,' he said instead. 'For being so great with my parents.'

'I liked them,' she said, and kissed him. 'I'm glad they came. It was good to meet them. And I have the feeling that Elle might just talk your father round...'

CHAPTER ELEVEN

THREE WEEKS LATER, Kelly had a half day. She'd been too busy to notice during the morning, but she felt odd. Queasy.

Probably low blood sugar, she told herself. She was meeting her sister for lunch, so it would be at least another half an hour until they ate. She went to the kiosk by the staff canteen to buy a cereal bar to tide her over, but the scent of the coffee made her feel even more queasy.

It wasn't until she was on the Tube and the cereal bar had done nothing to settle her stomach that the likely reason hit her.

No.

Ridiculous.

Of course she couldn't be pregnant. She and Luc had used protection whenever they'd made love.

But contraception wasn't always one hundred per cent effective.

She swallowed hard. Her period was late, but that was probably due to all the stress she'd been under lately—wasn't it?

Though the idea wouldn't leave her. Especially because the scents in the cafe where she met Susie made her feel even queasier than she'd felt in the hospital.

'Are you all right, Kel?' Susie asked.

'Course I am,' Kelly fibbed. This wasn't something she was ready to discuss with anyone. Not until she'd reassured herself that she was being ridiculous. She managed to keep the conversation light until Susie left to pick the boys up from school, and then she headed for a nearby supermarket and bought a pregnancy test. Not wanting to wait until she got home, she went to the toilet in the supermarket. Thankfully, the cubicles were all empty, so she didn't feel guilty about taking her time. She took a deep breath. This would reassure her that everything was fine and she was panicking over nothing.

She did the test, and watched the screen. A little square box appeared at the left hand side of the screen to show her that the test was working. Another appeared; another; and then the final one to say that the test was over.

Was she or wasn't she?

Time slowed down, and every second felt

like a minute. But finally the word flashed up on the screen. Absolutely definite.

Pregnant.

Oh, help.

What did she do now?

This wasn't part of the deal. Her marriage to Luc was supposed to be in name only—something that wasn't real. Except over the last few weeks they'd moved towards a rather different relationship. Friendship plus physical attraction. Did that really equal love?

But this pregnancy was a real game-changer. They couldn't pretend anything, any more. They had to face the reality.

She had absolutely no idea how Luc would react.

Would he insist on making their marriage permanent, for the sake of the baby? Would he expect to be part of the baby's life if they stuck to their original plan and had a quick divorce after a few months? Would he ask her to have a termination?

Kelly didn't think he'd choose the last option. She didn't want that, either. But as for their future… She had absolutely no idea what she really wanted, either. Her head was too much in panic mode now she knew she was pregnant.

She and Simon had planned to start trying for a baby—a much-wanted addition to their family who would be so very deeply loved. But she and Luc weren't in that position. His parents had been surprisingly kind and accepting, but she was pretty sure that Eleonora had had to talk them round to the idea; her first conversation with Vittoria, on Luc's laptop, had been awkward in the extreme. Would the baby change things? Would the news make things better, or would it be an extra complication?

And if the baby was a boy and the King didn't change the succession rules, that meant the baby she was carrying would be second in line to the throne. She and Luc would both be trapped; they'd both have to give up the careers they'd worked so hard to build. And no way would he be able to follow his dream of setting up his cardiac clinic.

She stared at the test stick. Given that it was digital, there was absolutely no way she'd misread it.

Pregnant.

All the way back to Luc's house, her mind was in a whirl.

'Are you all right, *bella*?' Maria asked when she walked in.

'Fine,' Kelly fibbed. 'Just a bit tired.' And she had no idea how to tell Luc.

She picked at her food that night, and he noticed. 'What's wrong? I know you met your sister for lunch. Susie and the baby are all right, aren't they?'

'Yes.' It wasn't Susie's baby who was the issue. It was theirs.

He frowned. 'Whatever's upset you, is it something I can help with?'

She blew out a breath. 'Luc, we need to talk. In private.'

'Now you're worrying me.'

He was going to be a lot more worried when she told him the news, she thought.

When she didn't answer, he said, 'OK. Let's go for a drive.'

'No.' This was going to be a shock to him, and driving wouldn't be sensible. 'Let's go for a walk in the garden.'

'If that's what you want, sure.'

Right at the bottom of the garden was a fountain; next to it was a wrought-iron bench. They sat down, and Luc waited patiently until Kelly was ready to talk.

She took a deep breath. 'There isn't an easy way to say this. I know we didn't plan it and we took precautions—but I'm pregnant.'

His expression was utterly inscrutable. 'How pregnant?'

'I'm a couple of weeks late.'

'And your cycle's regular?'

She nodded. 'Every twenty-eight days. Practically to the hour. We've both been busy since we came back from New York so I didn't notice I was late. It didn't even occur to me until today, when I felt a bit off-colour and then the smells in the cafe made me feel a bit sick. I thought I was being ridiculous, and then I realised my period was late.'

'Have you told anyone else?'

She shook her head. 'I didn't even tell Susie of my suspicions. I did a test on the way home—and I thought you ought to be the first to know.'

He was going to be a father.

The world spun for an instant.

He really hadn't expected Kelly to tell him this. And he had no clue about whether she was shocked or pleased or *anything*. They hadn't even discussed children. Their marriage was supposed to be in name only—except he'd changed the terms when he'd made love to her on their wedding night.

'Thank you for telling me first.' He paused.

'If my calculations are right, this is a honeymoon baby.'

'That's what I thought, too. Conceived in New York.' She swallowed hard. 'So, what now?'

'We're married,' he said. 'Our baby is legitimate. And, as he or she is my child, the baby will be a prince or princess.' And that changed everything. The baby would need his protection. He needed to make things right. He looked at her. 'So perhaps we should forget the few months we originally planned.'

'You mean, wait until after the baby arrives before we have our quiet divorce?'

'I mean, forget the divorce altogether. We're going to be parents, Kelly.'

'And what happens when your father finds out about the baby? If Elle has been trying to persuade him to change his mind about the succession rules, this baby…' Her voice tailed off and she stared at him.

'As things stand right now, then the baby will be second in line to the throne. If Babbo does decide to change the rules, the baby will still be fifth in line—it will be Elle, Alessio, Anna, me and then our baby, and then Giu.'

She raked a hand through her hair. 'Which means we're both trapped. We can't continue working here at Muswell Hill Memorial Hospital.'

'Not necessarily,' he said. He'd already disrupted her life so much. He needed to do the right thing and let her choose what she wanted to do. 'What do *you* want?'

'I…' She shook her head. 'I don't know. I hadn't even considered this might happen.'

'But you'd planned to have children with Simon.'

She looked away. 'Simon isn't here any more.'

Had she reached the stage where she was ready to move on and make a new life for herself? Or was she still in mourning? Luc had no idea. But now his head was clearing from the shock of the news and he knew exactly what he wanted from his life. He wanted Kelly and he wanted their baby.

'I need time to think about this,' she said. She looked him straight in the eye. 'What do *you* want?'

Crunch point.

If he told her that his feelings towards her had changed, would she be relieved or would she back away?

'I think we should stay married,' he said.

'For the baby's sake.'

Her tone was flat and he couldn't read her

expression. He could pussyfoot around the situation; then again, he'd always hated the intricacies of diplomacy. He preferred to tell it like it was. Telling her the truth couldn't make things any worse. 'Your life as my queen would be very different,' he said. 'And it wouldn't be what you'd signed up for. I know that. But, baby or no baby, I still don't want to be king. I want to be a cardiac surgeon. And I happen to like being married to you.'

'Because I'm safe?'

Did she really have no idea how he felt about her? 'Remember the song I sang at our wedding reception? I meant every word,' he said. 'I don't want to stay married to you for the baby's sake—I want to stay married to you for mine. I've fallen in love with you over the last couple of months, Kel. I thought I'd forgotten what love feels like, but being with you and waking up with you in my arms every morning makes the world feel like a much better place. And I know why. It's because I love you.'

She looked utterly shocked.

Did that mean that she hadn't guessed? Or did it mean that she didn't feel the same way about him and was horrified to think that he loved her?

He pressed on. 'I know you'll always love

Simon, and I don't intend to supplant him, but love stretches, Kelly. I hope you can learn to love me, too, to make our marriage a real one and make a family with me. But I'm not going to put pressure on you. I know I come with complications.' His royal lifestyle was the reason why Rachel had left him. Would it be the same for Kelly? The press had been horrible to her on the news of their marriage; although they'd weathered that particular storm, had it made her wary about how her life would be with him in the future?

'I'll give you as much time as you need to think, and I'll support whatever decision you make. But, even if you don't want me to be part of your life, I want to be part of the baby's life and give you all the support I can.'

She said nothing, and Luc felt sick. Maybe he shouldn't have declared himself after all. Maybe the past was just about to repeat itself.

'I'll give you time to think about what you want,' he said again, rising to his feet. 'Or to talk to someone you trust. Your mum, your sister, your best friend. No pressure.'

To make their marriage a real one and make a family with him.

And he hoped she'd learn to love him.

But was that how he really felt, or was he

only saying that because of the baby—because the baby would be a royal heir?

Kelly hadn't thought herself ready to move on, yet. And there was only one place she could go right now: only one person she could speak to.

'I need to go out,' she said.

'I'll get Gino to drive you.'

She could see that he was holding himself in check and trying not to smother her. 'Thank you, Luc. For giving me time,' she said, and reached out to squeeze his hand.

It didn't take long to drive to the church where Simon was buried. She'd had Gino stop to buy flowers on the way; and she knelt on the ground in front of the gravestone while she arranged them in the vase.

'I miss you,' she said. 'And I wish we could've had the chance to grow old together. But it wasn't to be.' She sat down properly and wrapped her arms around her knees. 'If I'd been the one to die, I would've wanted you to find someone else. Not to replace me, but to share your life and love you, the way you deserve to be loved, because I wouldn't have wanted you to be lonely. And I'm pretty sure that's the way you feel—felt—about me.' She dragged in a breath. 'I've met someone. We liked each other right from the start. We became friends. And we got married to solve a problem for both of us—to show his dad that he was committed to a life in medicine, being a heart surgeon; and to stop everyone trying to find me a new partner. Except it didn't quite work like that.'

Over the weeks of their marriage, it had changed.

'It didn't stay being a marriage in name only. He says he loves me, Simon, and I believe him. And I… I think I love him.' Now she'd said it out loud, it felt real. 'We're having a baby. It wasn't planned—but he's going to be as good a dad as you would've been. He's got a niece and nephew who adore him, and he's great with Jacob and Oscar. There's a bit of me that's scared he only loves me because I'm carrying his heir, but it's time for me to take a risk. To stop grieving and live again.'

Finally she could give herself permission to move on.

'I'll always love you and you'll always be part of me. But I want to make a life with Luc. Be his partner, be a cardiologist, and be the best mum I can be to our baby.' She smiled and stood up again. 'I guess I need to have a serious talk with Luc now. I won't ever forget you, and I'll always stay in touch with your family. That won't change.' She pressed her hand on the top of the gravestone. 'Wish me luck. We're still going to have to persuade Luc's dad that he's a heart surgeon rather than a future king. And I'm definitely not a queen. But we'll get there.'

Gino drove her back to Luc's house. When she walked through the front door, she could hear that he was playing the piano. Bach, the same kind of music he operated to: which gave her a clue that he was trying to think, to work out a solution to their situation. She tapped on the door of his office and went inside; he stopped playing as soon as she walked in.

'That sounded great,' she said. 'You don't have to stop.'

'Are you OK? Do you need anything?' he asked.

'Yes—and yes,' she said.

He looked faintly nervous. 'What do you need?'

'I need you to be honest with me.' She walked over to him and nudged him to budge over on the piano stool. 'I went to Simon's grave.'

'Uh-huh.' She could tell he was doing his best to keep his voice neutral, but it was obvious that he was on tenterhooks.

'What you said about loving me. Did you

mean it, or are you saying that because of the baby?'

'I meant it,' he said. 'It isn't just about the baby. Remember you said I needed to see things from my dad's side? Knowing that I'm going to be a father makes me realise that I want our child to grow up being loved and valued for their own sake, not because they'll be my heir. And that's how I feel about my wife. I want her to know I love her and value her for herself, not because she's pregnant with the potential second in line to the throne.' He took her hand. 'I love you, Kelly. For who you are, not what you represent.' He dropped a kiss into her palm and closed her fingers over it.

'You love me.'

'I love you for you. While you were gone, I took a hard look at my life. I know what I want. But I also know I need to be fair and give you the choice, not pressure you into doing what you think you ought to do.'

She nodded. 'What you said about love stretching. You're right. I'm finally ready to move on. And what I need is you.' She swallowed hard. 'Because somewhere along the way I fell in love with you, too. Waking up to every new day in your arms sounds just about perfect to me. I want to share my life with you and our baby—to make a family.'

'Married for real,' he said.

'Married for real,' she echoed. 'It's early days, but I think our family needs to know about the baby. We kept them in the dark about getting married and that was a huge mistake. We need to prove to them that we won't do that again, so we'll trust them with the news. And I think we need to go to Bordimiglia and have a very frank conversation with your dad.'

'Sort it out once and for all.' Luc looked at her. 'What if my father says he won't change the succession rules?'

'Then you get to be King. But if that happens, then when you're King, *you* can change the rules,' she said. 'Maybe you can work out a compromise where you share the royal duties with Elle and Giu, and get time to do some part-time work as a cardiac surgeon as well. You can have the best of both worlds.'

'Compromise.' He looked at her thoughtfully. 'And you're prepared for the media circus when we officially announce your pregnancy?'

'Yes—because I know you'll be by my side and I can handle anything with your help.'

'You're sure about this?' he checked.

'I'm sure about this. I love you,' she said simply.

'I love you, too,' he said. 'And we'll go to Bordimiglia on our next days off. Be open with my parents. And then face whatever happens next—together.'

'Together,' she agreed.

EPILOGUE

Ten months later

'You have everything you need, *bella*?' Umberto asked.

'We do, Babbo. *Grazie,*' Kelly said, and hugged him.

'I'm glad you're having Giacomo christened here in Bordimiglia. Of course, we would have come to London if you'd wanted us to,' Umberto said.

'But we're following the tradition and having him christened in the same place as his father, his grandfather, and every great-grandfather as far back as you can trace your family,' Kelly said with a smile.

'Tradition is good,' Umberto said to his son.

'Agreed. But I'm glad you've modernised the monarchy and Eleonora is taking over from you at the end of the summer,' Luc said.

He cradled his son tenderly, talking directly to him. 'Girl power is good. You tell your *nonno.*'

Obligingly, Giacomo gurgled.

'That's our boy.' With a grin, Luc handed his son over to Umberto.

Umberto smiled. 'My beautiful grandson. I wonder if he'll grow up to be as challenging as you, Luc?'

'He'll grow up to be himself,' Luc said. 'And I expect we'll fight like mad when he's a teenager. But I will teach him that family and love are the two most important things, and everything else is about negotiating a good compromise.'

'Compromise.' Umberto smiled. 'Your mother can't wait for you to come back to Bordimiglia next year to set up the new cardiac hospital, when your trial has finished. And it's going well?'

'It is.' Luc smiled at Kelly. 'Obviously I can't talk about any of my patients.'

'But I can,' Kelly said. 'My brother-in-law and niece are on the trial, and they're doing well. Thanks to Luc, I'm a lot less worried about their future.'

'I'm glad. And now I understand what you do in an operating theatre,' Umberto said. 'Seeing that video diary of your patient, how that poor man was breathless and could barely walk across the room, and then after you operated on him he was training to run a marathon—that is truly amazing.'

'It's good to be able to give someone a second chance at making the most of their life,' Luc said. 'And thank you for letting me do that instead of making me give it up to take over from you.'

'Your sister will be a better queen than you would have been a king. And it's right that she should get the chance to do that,' Umberto said. 'And your family will always be welcome to stay with us here, Kelly. They won't have to rely on video calls.'

'*Grazie.*' Kelly smiled at him.

'And now, *duchessa*, I think we're ready for church,' Luc said. As he'd predicted, Kelly wasn't officially a princess, but his father had bestowed the title of Duchess upon her.

'Back to your *mamma*, little one—though all your grandparents, aunts and uncles are going to be demanding cuddles later,' Umberto said, and handed the baby back to Kelly. Luc put his arm round Kelly's shoulder, and together they walked from the castle to the chapel and posed in the doorway for the media before walking down the aisle and sitting in the pew, waiting for the christening ceremony to begin.

'Old traditions and a new family,' Luc said softly.

'Old traditions and a new family,' Kelly echoed.

* * * * *

*If you enjoyed this story, check out
these other great reads from
Kate Hardy*

Carrying the Single Dad's Baby
Unlocking the Italian Doc's Heart
Their Pregnancy Gift
Christmas with Her Daredevil Doc

Available now!